SHADOW OF THE GALLOWS

 SCHOLASTIC

Scholastic Children's Books,
Euston House, 24 Eversholt Street,
London, NW1 1DB, UK

A division of Scholastic Ltd
London ~ New York ~ Toronto ~ Sydney ~ Auckland
Mexico City ~ New Delhi ~ Hong Kong

Published in the UK by Scholastic Ltd, 2008

ISBN 978 1407 10366 2

Printed and bound by Bookmarque Ltd, Croydon, Surrey

2 4 6 8 10 9 7 5 3 1

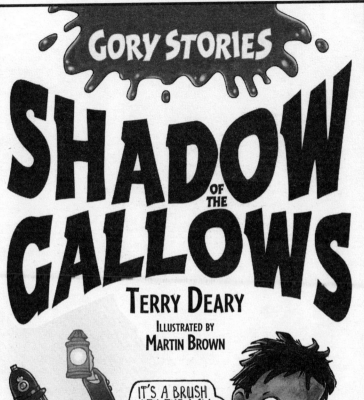

GORY STORIES

SHADOW OF THE GALLOWS

TERRY DEARY

ILLUSTRATED BY
MARTIN BROWN

IT'S A BRUSH WITH THE LAW

INTRODUCTION

When our story starts Queen Victoria was on the throne. I hope it was a very strong throne because Queen Victoria had a big bottom and a shaky seat would soon shatter under her weight.

Of course when someone says she was 'on the throne' it doesn't mean she spent her life sitting on a golden chair. She probably just spent a day or so every year sitting on the throne. 'On the throne' means she was the Queen at the time. So, why do people say a king or queen is 'on the throne' when they hardly ever were? I haven't a clue ... and I haven't a throne either.

Victoria had been happily married to Prince Albert for 17 years and they'd had nine children. When he died, in 1861, she dressed in black and became as miserable as a moping moggy that'd lost its milk. She just shut herself away from the people of Britain.

She was NOT popular. In fact a few people would quite like to have seen her dead as a duck's toenail ... as you'll see in this story.

It was all very well being a misery monarch but she was getting paid and not doing her job. Meanwhile millions of her poor people were suffering in the slimy slums of cities like London and Edinburgh. The poor who had nothing ended up in the wicked workhouses. Millions more had starved when their precious potatoes perished in Ireland between 1845 and 1849 ... and the Irish never quite forgave her for ignoring them. Would you?

If you DID get a job in Victoria's cities it would be a hard life – so hard it would probably kill you before you turned 30.

Of course you could always take to crime to make some money. You just had to make sure you didn't get caught because the punishments were painful. Flogged or sent to awful Australia, locked in a stinking cell or trotting along a treadmill.

Aha! You cry. What is a treadmill? Well I'll tell you, since I am so kind. It was like a huge hamster wheel for humans. You walked and walked and went nowhere. At the end of the day you were worn out and your legs ached till you thought they'd drop off. A bit like doing a cross-country lesson at school.

If your crime was bad enough you could end up swinging on the end of a rope ... and I don't mean by your hands.

Victoria's Britain was a pleasant place to live ... if you had money and weren't moping like the Queen. For most it was misery.

You don't want to have a miserable story though, do you? So let's look at the tale of a rich girl, shall we? Her name was Rachel Mackay.

6

Back in Edinburgh in 1868 they used to hang people in front of cheering crowds in the Old Town. The hangings were like a party. People brought picnics to watch men and women swing from the gallows. They listened to the victims confess their crimes and beg to God to forgive them.

The gallows were known as Calcraft's Toilet, because Master William Calcraft was Queen Victoria's chief hangman. His gallows were known as his toilet. Charming.

Rachel was only eight years old when she saw Mr Calcraft at work. Her mother took her all the way to Glasgow to see Doctor Edward William Pritchard hang for murdering his wife. Years later Rachel still remembered the excitement and the cheering as the evil man met his end.

But this is not just Rachel's story – the story really starts back in 1856 in Dundee. It starts with the birth of a baby…

A BUNDLE, A BOTTLE, A BAIRN

1856

Ethel Scrogg hurried over the dark and slimy cobbles with a bundle in her arms. The baby was wrapped in a rough woollen blanket and it whimpered.

There was some light from the taverns along the way but she was soon lost. A sailor with a red handkerchief around his neck stumbled out of the Blue Bell Inn and almost crashed into Ethel. 'Sorry, hinny,' he slurred.

'Can you help me?' the woman asked.

He peered into her young face – a long face with long teeth just a little like a horse. Not a pretty face but a strong one with fierce eyes. 'Help you? Are you a beggar? You don't look like a beggar … that shawl looks far too fine.'

She shook her head angrily. 'I am not asking for money. I simply want to know the way to Harbour Row.'

'Ooooh! You don't want to go to Harbour Row!' he moaned.

'I DO want to go to Harbour Row,' she snapped, 'or I wouldn't be asking the way!'

'I mean a fine lady like YOU does NOT want to go to a place like Harbour Row!' the sailor said, suddenly sober.

Something in Ethel Scrogg snapped. When that

happened her dark eyes seemed to glow red. 'Just tell me how to get to Harbour Row or I'll call a peeler and have you arrested for attacking me!'

'I didn't attack you!' the sailor gasped.

'I don't care. The police will believe *me*, not some drunken layabout like you. Now are you going to tell me where Harbour Row is or do I have to blow my police whistle?' she asked fiercely. She pulled out a silver whistle that hung around her neck and put it to her lips.

'Where did you get that from?' the man spluttered. 'Don't blow it for the love of God!'

'Harbour Row!' she roared at him.

He used the end of his sleeve to wipe across his dripping nose. 'You're in it,' he snarled and staggered away to the next tavern in the row of pitiful houses.

A wind blew off the North Sea and rattled the Blue Bell Inn signs. A small cottage showed a candle in the window. Ethel squinted through the dust and cobwebs at the row of cradles inside. A thin woman rocked herself in a chair by the hearth and supped from a dark green bottle. This was the place.

Ethel knocked at the front door to the cottage and the woman took a long time to answer. When she did her thin face looked out fiercely. 'What do you want?' Then she noticed Ethel's fine shawl and her face softened. 'Hello, my dear,' she crooned. 'What can I do for a fine lady like you?'

'Miss Bruce? Miss Kitty Bruce?'

'Who wants to know?'

Ethel didn't answer the question. Instead she said, 'I

understand you're a baby farmer?'

Miss Bruce's eyes turned tiger bright and she looked down the street. 'I am *not* ... don't call me that. Do you want the law down on me, foolish child?' She reached out a claw hand and pulled Ethel inside the dirty hallway and led her into a room full of cots. It stank of sour baby milk and gin. Ethel wrinkled her nose.

'Sorry, Miss Bruce ... I meant to say you care for babies, don't you?'

'I find poor orphan lambs new homes with caring parents,' Kitty Bruce said in a gentle voice. 'Do you have another one for me?'

Ethel Scrogg held out the whimpering bundle. 'I have this child ... I ... I am not able to care for it. I need to go to Edinburgh and leave the child behind.'

TWENTY POUNDS

'Twenty? I thought you charged five.'

Kitty shrugged softly and looked up into Ethel's face. 'You have a baby with no father. Now you want to go back to Edinburgh to marry some rich man ... but he would never marry you if he knew you had this baby, would he?'

Ethel's long top teeth chewed at her bottom lip. 'Ten pounds,' she murmured.

'So I am right,' Kitty cackled. 'In fact you may already have met the man ... he is waiting for you in Edinburgh. Twenty pounds.'

'Fifteen.'

'He proposed to you ... didn't know you were with child ... you made up a story about visiting an aunt in Dundee and came up here to have the child. Am I right?'

'No,' Ethel said, alarmed at how much the baby farmer guessed. Did she have many women come to her this way?

No, she didn't. Kitty Bruce was not a clever woman or a mind-reader. She simply knew Ethel Scrogg's Dundee aunt. She heard Ethel's story long before she arrived on Kitty's dusty doorstep. Ethel would not often be beaten in her wicked life but she had no chance against Kitty Bruce ... not then. Later she would take her revenge. Terrible revenge...

'I'm sure he's a fine gentleman and it's worth twenty pounds to be free to marry him. Is he a gentleman?' Kitty asked.

Ethel raised her chin proudly, 'He is a Colonel in the British Army. But when his father dies he'll be a Lord … Lord Mackay!' Then she chewed her lip again, knowing she had made a terrible mistake.

'A *Lord,* eh? Then that'll be fifty pounds.'

'Twenty, not a penny more,' Ethel snapped back … more annoyed with herself at giving so much away. 'There are plenty of other baby farmers in the region.'

'Don't use that word.'

'Women who care for babies then,' Ethel said with a sneer. 'Twenty pounds.'

Kitty Bruce sighed and tried to look defeated. Really she was pleased to take four times what other mothers paid to be rid of their brats. 'Twenty pounds and I'll find him a loving home … and no one will know where he came from,' she added quietly.

Ethel pulled out a purse and counted out twenty sovereigns. It was money well spent. 'Does the bairn have a name?' Kitty asked.

'The bairn? Oh … Bairn will do. It hasn't been christened. Call it … call it *Bairn.*' Ethel looked around the room. There was only the sound of the fire crackling. 'The babies are quiet,' she said.

'Well fed and happy,' Kitty sighed, 'just as yours will be.'

Ethel nodded, handed over her baby in its shawl and walked quickly to the door. She didn't look back as she fled from the sour-smelling house.

Kitty Bruce cradled the child. The baby farmer smiled and murmured, 'You haven't seen the last of this baby or me. Oh, no, Miss Scrogg. Not by a long way. We'll meet again, some chilly day! Heh!'

The baby began to whine softly. Kitty reached for a bottle and poured a mixture on to a spoon. 'A drop of laudanum will settle you like all the rest,' she said as gently as a dove. The baby took it. The baby farmer added a little of the liquid from her own green bottle. 'And a little gin to help you sleep,' she added. The baby called Bairn gave a small gasp but had to swallow the gin rather than choke. It screwed up its tiny face but its eyelids were heavy. It slept.

Ethel Scrogg slept on the night train back to Edinburgh. It rattled and shook down the line. Cows and sheep in the fields fled in terror when its whistle screamed.

But Ethel slept. Her trip to Dundee was a success. Her mistake was behind her now. The child would be better off and, more important, Ethel Scrogg would be better off.

Ethel dreamed of being a queen among the rich ladies of Edinburgh … it only needed old Lord Mackay to die and for her to marry his son, Arthur.

When the train steamed into one of Edinburgh's Waverley stations the next morning a man of about 30 years old stood waiting on the platform. If Ethel's chin was a little too long then he had hardly any chin at all. He hid it under a flowing beard and managed to look splendid and handsome in his dark blue uniform.

He saluted Ethel and took her bag from her. They walked to the horse-drawn carriages at the station entrance. The sharp, smoky smell of Edinburgh met Ethel's long curving nose. The reek of Edinburgh – Old Reekie as the farmers of Fife called the city. 'You have lost weight, Ethel,' Colonel Mackay said with surprise as he helped her into his carriage. 'The Dundee air must have done you good.'

She smiled. 'It did. So when do we marry, Arthur?'

'Soon, my duckling … the army is posting me to India next month and I want to take you with me as my bride!'

> When he says the Army is 'posting' him he doesn't mean they are wrapping him in brown paper, sticking on a stamp and pushing him through a pillar box. You are not stupid enough to think that, are you? Oh, and when he calls her 'Duckling' it doesn't mean she is a feathered thing with a yellow bill. That's just quackers.

'India?' she asked. 'Very hot, India.'

'But very rich – a British soldier can make his fortune there.'

'You *have* a fortune, Arthur … or you will have when your father dies,' his bride-to-be said.

'A man can never have too much money.' Arthur chuckled.

'Or a woman.' Ethel smiled.

'Anyway … out in India they used to burn a widow alive when her husband died. The British put a stop to it. The Indians are *not* happy. There's a mutiny in the air. They need me.'

Ethel sighed. 'Then we must go, my love … and if you *die* at least I know they won't burn me!'

'If I die you'll be a very rich woman, hah!' Arthur Mackay barked. 'We'll both be rich when poor old Pa hops the twig.'

The carriage climbed the hill from the station. A fine gold-trimmed carriage with a coachman in green and gold. It trotted along Princes Street and up into the fine houses of the New Town. The filth of the Old Town was left behind them. Ethel had been born in that old part of town but had used her cunning to escape. Now the reward was in her grasp – she took the hand of Arthur Mackay. She felt like Cinderella – Arthur would never be Prince Charming, but he would do. Ethel smiled. 'And how is your father?'

'Not well – not well at all. In fact he may die any day now … and you could be travelling to India as Lady Mackay.'

'Great,' she muttered under her breath.

'What was that my sweet?' he asked.

'Great … pity,' she sighed. 'Life can be terribly cruel.'

But she had a smile on her face as she turned to look out of the carriage window.

SWADDLING, SELLING AND SOOT

1862

Kitty Bruce took special care of Bairn. She didn't sell him off to the first childless, child-seeking couple that came along like the other babies in her care. She kept him.

She wrapped him tight in blankets for the first year of his life.

> Yes, I know, all mothers used to wrap their babies in tight 'swaddling' clothes to stop them hurting themselves for the first couple of months of their lives. But that wasn't Kitty Bruce's plan ... as you will see.

She fed him laudanum and gin to make him sleep at night and gin and laudanum so he slept through the day. The baby was hardly ever hungry and passed the days in a daze.

When at last she set him free he soon became bright and strong. He was walking in no time and quickly learned to talk. (When he chattered too much Kitty Bruce just fed him more laudanum to slow him down.)

But his body – ah, his poor body was stunted like a flower in a drought. He would grow strong and he would grow healthy ... but he would never grow very tall. 'Perfect!' Kitty cackled as she watched the boy run in the fields and climb trees faster than a monkey. She supped at her gin and nodded.

In the fields Bairn met other children and they shared their stories. That's where Bairn first heard the story of Dick Whittington. He went home that evening with his eyes glowing. 'If a poor boy like Dick Whittington can get to the top then so can I. One day I'll be Lord Mayor of Dundee!' he told Kitty Bruce.

'Aye, and one day I'll be the richest woman in Dundee,' she nodded.

Bairn scowled at her. 'I wasn't being silly, Aunt Kitty.' He was just five years old but he knew when adults were poking fun.

She supped her gin and wiped her mouth. 'I wasn't being silly either,' the woman hissed. 'One day we'll be at the very top ... side by side!'

She was right! One day they would. Sometimes your dreams come true ... but not in the way you think...

***

By the time he was six years old Bairn was ready. He was no bigger than a child of four, 'But you're bright as a button, aren't you Bairn? Bright as a box full of buttons.'

He grinned and nodded. 'Yes, Aunt Kitty. And I'm going to be the greatest man in Scotland ... one day. Not Dundee ... the whole of Scotland.'

If Bairn spent too many hours asleep at least he spent them dreaming. And dreams can take you anywhere, they can take you to India ... but just as easily they can take you to the gallows. Bairn's dreams burned fierce as a fire of Newcastle coal.

One morning Kitty Bruce gave him a fine breakfast of

porridge made with milk, not water. She packed some cheese and bread and dressed him in a good suit and some new boots. Then she told him, 'It's time you paid your old Aunt Kitty back for the years she's spent feeding you. Time for you to get a job.'

'What sort of job?' Bairn asked. 'I'm a bit small to be a shop boy – I can't reach the shelves.'

'No money in shops,' Kitty said as she hobbled down the rough road to Dundee station. 'No, I thought you could become a chimney sweep.'

'Dick Whittington wasn't a sweep. Is there money in sweeping?' he asked.

'Well, you can get to the top,' Kitty joked.

It wasn't a very good joke, but Kitty wasn't a very good woman. Only great people like me can make great jokes.

'But you can't get far in Dundee,' she sighed. 'We need to take you to Edinburgh. They have the Old Town there with the most twisted chimneys you ever saw – always clogging up and needing a sweep. And there is the New Town with the finest houses in the world, full of rich folk who pay well to keep their fires blazing. Oh, yes, Edinburgh's the place to be and sweeping is the job to have,' she said as she paid for a ticket in a covered carriage.

Kitty Bruce made a good living as a baby farmer. There were always people happy to pay her to take their babies away – and always people ready to buy a baby from her. So for each baby she was paid twice. They cost little to keep – watery porridge and laudanum didn't cost much. And she didn't spend a lot – gin was cheap. I don't want you thinking Kitty was a 'poor' woman. Just greedy. Always wanting more. You must know people like that? Anyway, Kitty could certainly afford a good seat on the train.

The train whistle blew and the massive wheels clanked and skidded as it pulled from the station and headed south. It was the first time Bairn had left Dundee and he marvelled at the mountains and the rivers, the strange towns and the country villages. Harbour Row was poor and sluggish as the sewer that ran down the middle of the lane. But the train huffed through bustling places as busy as anthills … the sort of places where Bairn could feel the thrill of adventure.

They crossed the River Tay at Perth, crawling over a shivering wooden bridge, so feeble it felt as if a jerk would send them crashing into the dark waters. The new iron bridge ran alongside them and it would soon be finished. 'That's being built so the Queen will be safe when she takes the train to Balmoral,' Kitty sniffed. 'We can risk our lives on a wooden bridge but the Queen has to have an iron one.'

'Is it good to be Queen then?' he asked.

'Sometimes.' Kitty sighed.

The palace at Linlithgow made him gape as they

rattled past. 'Mary Queen of Scots lived there,' Kitty Bruce said. 'Sad lady.'

'Why was she sad? Living in a house like that? I thought it was good to be a Queen. Did she have smoky chimneys?' Bairn asked.

'She was sad because she was executed.'

'They hanged a fine lady who came from a palace like that?' the boy said in wonder.

'No ... fine ladies get their heads cut off. Only the poor like you and me get hanged, Bairn,' Kitty snorted.

'Is that's what's going to happen to us?' Bairn asked. 'Are we going to hang in Edinburgh?'

'I hope not,' the woman muttered. Anyone can hope ... but hope doesn't stop it happening.

'So is it better to get your head chopped off? Is that why they do it to ladies?'

Kitty Bruce sighed. 'When Mr Calcraft hangs a poor person he uses the short drop – it strangles you and you can take a long time to die. Other hangmen use the long drop, snap your neck and you go out like a candle in a gale.'

'But head-chopping is quicker?' asked Bairn.

'Ah, it *should* be. But poor Mary Queen of Scots met a clumsy axeman. He took three chops to get her head off. They say she cried out when the first blow nicked her neck. Nasty.'

The thought made Bairn go quiet for a while. What would it be like to kill a queen?

One day, dear reader, he would come close as a whisker to finding out. But I am jumping ahead with my story. Teasing you to make you read on. It's what writers do. If it annoys you then sorry ... it's my job.

Then the train took a curve and he saw the clear sky had a thick grey fog over it. 'What's that, Aunt Kitty?' he asked.

'Old Reekie ... that's the smoke that Edinburgh spits out every day,' she told him.

Bairn nodded wisely. 'I can see why they'd need plenty of sweeps then.'

***

Mr Georgio Grey was grey. His pale skin had seen so much soot that all the soap in Edinburgh couldn't wash him quite clean. He wore a fine tailcoat that was faded to dark grey and a white shirt that had dirtied to pale grey.

His grey hair was wild as one of his chimney brushes and now he smiled (with grey teeth) down on little Bairn. 'I see you've kept him small, Miss Bruce,' he said in a voice as soft and smooth as soot.

'Kept him small ... just the way you sweeps like them,' she nodded. 'Small but tough as wire. Bright too, aren't you, Bairn?'

'Bright as a box of buttons,' the boy replied.

'I'll take him,' Mr Grey said with a clap of his grimy hands.

'What will I have to do, sir?' Bairn asked politely.

'My business is to clean chimneys, as you know. We have brushes on poles and we shoves them up the chimneys, pulls them back down. Then we shovels the soot in the sacks and carries it off. Think you can do that?'

'Yes, sir.'

Mr Grey licked his pink lips … which weren't grey … and looked over his shoulder to check that no one was looking. 'But there is a little extra service we provides,' he said in a voice even softer than soot. He cleared his throat and leaned forward. 'There are some customers – the older customers – that don't believe the brushes gets the chimneys *really* clean. They like the chimneys swept the old way. Know what I mean?'

'No,' Bairn said shaking his head.

Mr Grey's voice was almost a whisper. 'They like to see a boy climb up the chimney and brush it out by hand. This is an extra service and they pay well for it. But my boys are getting too big for that job. We need a new young apprentice – a small lad … someone like you. Think you could do it, Bairn?'

'He climbs trees like a rabbit!' Kitty Bruce chuckled.

Mr Grey gave a grey frown. 'Can't say as I've ever seen a rabbit climb a tree, Miss Bruce,' he muttered.

'You know what I mean … hops up them, hops back down. Nimble as a cat.'

'A rabbit cat?' the sweep said and blinked at the thought.

'A *rabbit cat*. Which is why he's worth fifty pounds to you, Mr Grey,' Kitty Bruce smiled.

Mr Grey turned purple – a grey shade of purple. 'Fifty! I thought we agreed twenty-five when he was born.'

Kitty spread her hands. 'He's valuable to you, Mr Grey, and I spent a lot of time and money growing him to order. Special.'

'But *fifty* pounds for a boy!'

Kitty just smiled. 'Try getting one cheaper,' she said.

Mr Grey looked sulky. 'Could if I tried,' he grumbled.

The baby farmer just shook her head. 'You and I know it is against the law to send boys up chimneys. It has been for twenty years.'

Oh, dear, I feel like one of those school teachers that bore children till they fall asleep BUT I have to say Miss Bruce was not quite right. Sending boys up chimneys was banned in 1840 ... twenty-two years before. Another law, four years before that, in 1864, tried to ban it again. Of course it still went on, even though it was against the law. A bit like murder and robbery really.

'Twenty-five pounds for the boy,' Kitty Bruce smirked, 'And twenty-five for me to keep quiet.'

Mr Grey glared at her with his grey eyes. 'I'll have to work the boy hard to get my money back,' he said.

Kitty bowed her head. 'I don't mind that,' she said. 'I don't mind that at all. Now if we have a deal I need to visit someone else in Edinburgh while I'm down here.'

The sweep paid her the money and she kissed Bairn on the head. 'I'll be back from time to time to see you,' she said. 'There's still a lot of money to be made out of you, young man. An awful lot.'

She hurried from Mr Grey's house in the Old Town, past the narrow lanes they called wynds. Sullen men and sour women watched her from the shadows of the dark doorways – always dark, even at noon. Then they turned their eyes away – Kitty looked too poor to be worth robbing.

Children wept in the gutters and begged for scraps. Kitty hurried past. She walked over the North Bridge into the New Town and up

Princes Street. At the west end she turned into Charlotte Square and searched for a number she had written on a piece of paper.

The house was tall and handsome as Prince Albert himself, Kitty thought. She knew she wouldn't be welcome at the front door so she went to the end of the row and into the back lane. She walked past the carriage house and through the kitchen garden till she came to the back door. The house looked deserted but a kitchen maid answered her knock.

'Is this the house of Lord and Lady Mackay?' Kitty asked sweetly.

The maid wiped her nose on the back of her sleeve. 'Who wants to know?' she sniffed.

'An old friend.'

'Then an old friend ought to know His Lordship is serving in India with the Army. He won't be back for another six years – try again in 1868,' the maid sneered and slammed the door shut.

Kitty sighed. 'I can wait,' she said. 'The price will go on rising every year … but I can wait.'

*****

Bairn was given ragged old clothes to work in and his new suit and boots were put away.

He was shown into a cellar that had sacks of soot on the floor. 'This is where you sleep,' Mr Grey said.

'Sleep on what?' Bairn asked.

'On the sacks of soot, of course,' Mr Grey said.

'Ah,' Bairn nodded. 'Of course.' The door closed behind him. *Welcome to Edinburgh*, he thought. *Welcome to Edinburgh*.

The cellar was small and dark. But the boy's dreams just grew bigger and brighter.

'If I'm going to be a sweep I'm going to be the best sweep Edinburgh has ever seen. The very best.'

And he fell asleep with a smile on his thin, pale face.

SHADOWS, SILVER AND SLAVES

1868

Six years later there was a knock at the door of the house on Charlotte Square. It was a clear spring morning and the wind off the Lothian Hills was fresh.

A tall footman opened the door and looked down his nose at the strange, ugly woman who stood there. His uniform was dark green and had gold braid on the shoulders and the edges of the pockets. 'Back door,' he said sourly. 'Servants' door.'

'I haven't come to see the servants,' she said sweetly. 'I have come to see Lady Mackay. I heard she is back from India.'

The servant drew himself up to his full height. 'Her ladyship only sees people who have made an appointment. She has not said she is expecting anyone today.'

'She is not expecting me,' the woman said and the idea made her chuckle. 'She's not expecting me at all. I'll be quite a surprise in fact! But she *will* see me.'

The footman sighed. 'Give me your calling card and I will ask her ladyship if she is free.'

'People like me don't have fancy cards. And Lady Mackay's free – I'm the one who'll be charging,' the woman cackled. 'Tell her Kitty Bruce wants to see her.'

Sorry that is another dreadful joke isn't it? I warned you Kitty
Bruce made terrible jokes.

The footman nodded but closed the door and made her
wait on the doorstep. Kitty Bruce looked at the shiny door
sourly. 'The price has just gone up ... again,' she
muttered.

***

The next evening, there was a knock at the door of the
house in Chambers Street in the Old Town. It was a good
house and the owner was proud of the shining brass
knocker and the brightly painted door. A small brass
plate said, *Mr Georgio Grey – Master sweep.* Mr Grey
himself opened the door and let in the cool evening air. It
was dark in the street now. Six years on Mr Grey was a
little greyer. His hair and coat had faded to the colour of
his grey skin.

Six years on Bairn had grown, but not a lot. He
was almost as grey-skinned as his master but nothing
could dim the sparkle in his eyes or in his mind.
'I won't be a sweep forever,' he used to tell the other
apprentices ... the apprentices who *didn't* climb into the
chimneys. 'One day I'll be my own master and Mister
Grey can find another poor soul to climb the chimneys.
One day.'

'Mr Grey owns you,' one boy told Bairn.

Bairn shook his head. 'I've paid him back a hundred

times. He'll have to let me go when something better comes along.'

Bairn sat on the soot sack in the cellar and dreamed of marrying a rich merchant's daughter and becoming Lord Mayor ... that's how Dick Whittington had got on. Dreaming Bairn didn't hear the knock on the front door.

Life is funny like that. If he HAD heard the knock on the door, and gone to see who was there, the whole story would have been different. NO story in fact! Funny thing, life.

He didn't answer it as he usually did. Mr Grey did.

A shadowy figure stood there. A youth whose face was hidden under the broad brim of a hat. A slim youth. Slim as the shadows in the alleys that hid the beggars and the rats in the gutters, the footpads and the cats in the doorways, the mangy dogs rooting in the rubbish heaps.

The youth handed over two messages to the sweep master and said, 'Follow the orders exactly. Exactly. Then burn them.'

Then the shadowy figure ran off into the darkness and down the cobbles towards the South Bridge.

Mr Grey nodded his head and took the messages inside to read it in the light in the parlour.

He smiled. Of course it was secret. Of course sending a boy up a chimney was against the law. Of course the house owner sent a servant. The first slip of paper explained what the owner wanted – chimneys cleaned the best way, with a boy – but didn't give the owner's name. The paper was wrapped round a golden sovereign. The second piece gave only the address. No one could link the two pieces of paper so no one could link the house owner and the law-breaking.

Mr Grey gave his soot-soft chuckle and burned the paper. Then he went down into the cellar.

***

What's that I hear you say? You're tired of all this soot and sadness? Well this is where a girl enters our story. 'About time!' I hear you cry, 'Let's have a normal sort of girl'.

Rachel Mackay was maybe a little richer than normal child, but she was quite ordinary to look at. Her hair was long and dark and glowed like a chestnut – her maid brushed it every night and every morning to keep it shining and free from lice. Rachel's brown eyes were a little darker than her hair – like those of a young deer.

The evening after Mr Grey got his message Rachel sat in an armchair in her living room and shivered. The early spring evening was cool. Winter would be with Edinburgh a little while longer and the house still needed its fires. But you can't have a fire when there is a sweep in the chimney and there was a boy in the chimney that evening. So Rachel shivered.

There were terrible tales of careless servants lighting fires while a boy was still in the house chimneys. First the boy was roasted slowly and then he suffocated. His screams were muffled by the thick chimney walls and the thicker soot. Even without fires it was a dangerous job. Some boys got stuck and were smothered in the soft black soot. Others tumbled down from the top and smashed into the hearth in a pool of blackened blood. Mostly the danger was the fire. Of course that was why kind gentlemen in London passed laws and stopped the climbing boys. But the kind gentlemen in London were 400 miles away.

Rachel sat on an armchair and read a book. It was by the famous Scotsman, Sir Walter Scott, and it was an adventure set in Edinburgh.

He is such a famous writer they have built a monument to him in Edinburgh on Princes Street. The man who built the monument, George Meikle Kemp, died before it was finished. One dark night he fell into the Union Canal and drowned. I do think that's a sad little story, don't you? Funny, but sad. Sir Walter wrote very long books, but a young lady like Rachel had time to read long books.

Rachel heard a soft scraping from behind the canvas over the hearth – a canvas to stop falling soot spilling into the room. A face appeared from behind the canvas. A soot-smeared face with a pair of bright eyes peering out.

'Sorry, Miss,' the boy said. 'I'll sack up the soot and be out in no time.'

She threw down her book.

33

'I'm a sweep,' he said. He was thin as a chicken bone in a rat's nest.

'I *know* you're a sweep ... I can *see* you're a sweep! But why are you *in* the chimney? It's against the law! Does your master know?'

'Ha!' he laughed. 'It was Mr Grey that sent me.'

'He has no right,' Rachel shouted angrily. 'Why do you do it?'

'He'll beat me if I don't,' the boy cried.

'You are a slave,' the girl moaned. Then she remembered a song called *Rule Britannia* that she'd heard when the soldiers set sail to fight in the Crimea. 'Britons never, never, *never* shall be slaves.'

The boy stood in the hearth and grinned. 'Don't worry about me, Miss. When I'm thirteen, next year, I'll be finished as apprentice to Mr Grey and I can find another job. I'll be a great man ... like Dick Whittington.'

'Where's your cat?' Rachel snapped at the foolish boy. She rose to her feet, towering over Bairn. 'I cannot stand here and see a boy in slavery. Let me free you *now*!' she cried.

He scratched his head. 'I have to make a living,' he argued. 'I can't starve.'

'True,' she groaned and sank on to the sofa. In a moment she was back on her feet. 'The ornament!' she said pointing to the mantelpiece above his head.

It was the china figure of a white dog. 'What about it?'

'It was brought here by Mr Twist of High Street in the Old Town. He was moaning because he had to close the shop to deliver trinkets like this. He said he needs an errand boy – someone bright and careful … he sacked the last boy because he broke so many precious things.'

The sweep boy shrugged. 'The job will be gone by the time I'm free to leave Mr Grey,' he said.

There was a soft tap at the door. A grey man stood there. 'Excuse me, Miss Rachel. If the boy's finished I'll just take the sack away.' He wrung his grey hands. 'Sorry if I disturbs you, Miss.'

The girl stood up again and marched across to him. 'Take the sack – leave the boy. I am going to find him a new job.'

'I paid for him!' the master sweep whined.

Rachel fixed him with her hardest stare. 'Mr Grey, is it?'

'Yes, Miss.'

'Leave the boy or I will go to the police. Chief Inspector Gott is a friend of my family. When he hears about this boy … whatsisname?'

'Bairn, Miss.'

'When he hears about Bairn being *forced* to climb chimneys he will *arrest* you and you will spend a few years in jail. Would you like that?'

'No, it's a ten pound fine, Miss.'

'He will have you sent to jail if I demand it. Understand?'

'Yes, Miss.'

'Then Bairn stays,' she said with menace.

Rachel did 'menace' very well. You can try it some time. She would stand tall and raise her chin. She'd narrow her eyes and raise one eyebrow, then make her lips tight and thin. She looked magnificent. Menacing, but magnificent.

The man looked as if he wanted to argue but knew he was beaten. He picked up the bag of soot and took down the canvas. He looked like a whipped dog.

He turned and gave the boy a grey smile. 'Best of luck, young Bairn,' he said. 'You were always my best lad. You'll do well.'

He left.

The maid came in and jumped when she saw Bairn standing in the fireplace. 'I came to ask if you wanted the fire lit, Miss Rachel,' she said. 'I thought the sweeps had finished.'

'They *have*,' Rachel said. 'Light the fire then bring a bath. I want the footman to wash the boy till he's clean.'

'It'll take more than *one* bath to do that,' the maid muttered.

'As many as it takes,' Rachel said. 'And find him some clean clothes. He can sleep in the servants' attic tonight.'

'Yes, Miss Rachel,' the maid said and bobbed a curtsey to her mistress.

Rachel looked at the boy. 'Tomorrow will be the first step on a new road for you,' she said.

The boy grinned. Of course he didn't know it was the first step on a road that he may not want to walk on...

***

Mr William Twist had the face of an angel and the heart of a hangman. His friends called him Bill. Bill the Burglar. He was not much taller than Bairn but neat as a pin in his fine clothes. His head was bald as an egg and his ears sharp as the pixie ears you'll have seen in books. 'Yes, Miss Rachel,' he said. 'He'll make a fine shop boy. And he was a sweep, you say? Then he is simply perfect!'

The shop on the Edinburgh High Street was small but rather like the cave of Aladdin, packed with silver stuff from plates to pepper-pots, china vases and ornaments, ivory carvings and jade figures, paintings in fine frames and leather-bound books.

Rachel left Bairn in the care of the shopkeeper. 'Now, my boy, you will have a good life with me but you have to work for it.'

'I always work hard,' Bairn said. 'But what sort of work do you expect me to do?'

'Come into the back room. I'll lock the shop front door – there are lots of thieves around and you can't trust anyone,' he said and chuckled as if he'd cracked the funniest joke in the world. 'I will tell you how you can help to make us both very rich.' He locked the door and pulled down the blind. He frowned. 'I am rich now … but with a sweep boy to help I can make us rich as your friend, Miss Rachel. Maybe as rich as Queen Victoria! Come along and I'll tell you how we're going to do it…'

***

Two weeks later and the police were panicking. A burglar was raiding the richest houses in town and stealing valuables. Yet there were no broken locks on the doors or windows. It was almost as if the burglar could walk through walls and there was nothing the police could do to stop him.

Two weeks later a shadowy youth appeared at Bill Twist's door. The youth's face was hidden under the broad brim of a hat and his hand held a small piece of paper. It said:

23 George Street. Rich American. Silver dinner service in the dining room. Worth £100 at least. A friend.

'Who sent this?' Twist asked.

'A friend,' the youth whispered and hurried away into the shadows.

TERROR, TRINKETS AND TRAPS

Dr Joseph Bell was a clever man and, as the Queen's Doctor, was well known. On a chilly April evening he knocked on the door of the small room in the Central Police Station. Chief Inspector Gott cried, 'Come in!' The Doctor opened the door, shook his umbrella and placed it in the umbrella stand. The stand was made from the foot of an elephant.

> Lots of Victorian umbrella stands were made from the sawn-off feet of dead elephants. You probably knew that. I just felt like saying it.

In 1868 the Doctor was a neat man of just thirty years with eyes that never rested and lips that always held a small smile. 'I timed my visit well. See you got in just ten minutes ago,' the Doctor said brightly.

Chief Inspector Gott was a slow, heavy man with three chins more than most people. He made up for this extra weight by having less brain than most people. He scowled and looked at his pocket watch. He scowled again. 'How could you know that, Dr Bell? Eh, I say? How?'

'When you entered the station you asked for a cup of

tea. It would take ten minutes to boil the water, make the tea and serve you. It's still hot and you haven't had time to drink it.'

Gott's little eyes looked smug. 'Aha! Doctor, but how could you know I ordered my tea when I came in? I could have been sitting here all day. This could be my tenth cup of tea! You are guessing, Doctor. You can't *know* I've just come in.'

Doctor Bell shrugged. 'Your galoshes and umbrella are wet,' he said pointing to the elephant's foot.

'The bottoms of your trousers are still damp. It started raining a quarter of an hour ago. So you hurried back to the station and ordered a cup of tea to warm you up.'

The policeman slapped his pen on his desk and the nib splattered ink over the green-leather top. 'Oh, all right. You are a clever man. Maybe you can have my job and solve the crime in Edinburgh,' he snapped and his chins wobbled.

Doctor Bell grinned. 'Edinburgh police have so many excellent detectives – fine men like you – that you don't need me, Chief Inspector. I am just a humble doctor. I care for the sick bodies – you catch the ones with sick minds.'

Gott looked pleased with the thought. 'I do. Now, Doctor, have a seat and tell me how I can help you? Eh, I say? How?'

Joseph Bell leaned forward and spoke softly. 'Her Majesty Queen Victoria is due in Edinburgh soon. She is on her way to Balmoral. I will join her train when it stops at Waverley. When she is residing in Scotland I am her Doctor.'

'I know, I know.'

Bell's voice dropped still further. 'You have heard of the Fenian Brotherhood, of course?'

Gott nodded. 'American and Irish people who want to see a free Ireland. Ireland ruled by the Irish, not Queen Victoria and the English. Rebels who want to drive the British out,' he grunted. 'What has that to do with the Queen's visit to Scotland?'

'The Irish rebels have never forgiven Victoria for the famine that killed a million people, twenty years ago.

41

They can't win a war against the British Army but they *can* try to bring terror to our country,' the Doctor said.

Gott nodded. 'But London, not Edinburgh,' he argued.

The Doctor shook his head. 'Victoria herself is the target. There is a plot to attack her once she is away from the safety of London and her guards. They may try in Edinburgh.'

Gott's red face turned pale and his chins turned even paler. 'The disgrace of it! If the Queen were hurt when she passes through my patch. Eh, I say? What? How can I stop them?'

Joseph Bell spread his hands. 'This is top secret, Chief Inspector … but the British have a spy in the American Fenian Army … Henri Le Caron. He was able to tell us that Fenians have been ordered to attack Victoria … so we know they will try. But the Scottish Fenians can decide *how* they do it … where and when. We *don't* know that. We don't even know who the Scottish Fenians are. They could be anywhere in Scotland, plotting right now.'

Gott's chins were frozen in fear. 'I thought they were arrested last year. Their leader … Colonel Kelly was arrested in Manchester, wasn't he?'

Joseph Bell nodded. 'Those were Irish Fenians working in England. Kelly was being carried through Manchester in a police van when a gang of his friends attacked it and tried to free him. Police Sergeant Brett looked through the keyhole to see what was going on … just as they fired at the lock. He died. Three Irishmen were hanged for the murder … hanged in front of Manchester jail. They are calling them the Manchester Martyrs.'

'And there was that explosion in London,' Gott said slowly.

Doctor Joseph Bell nodded. 'The Fenians blew up a prison wall to set one of their friends free. It killed 12 people. Michael Barratt will hang next month for that. The Fenians think that attacking Victoria will frighten us into setting him free.'

Gott groaned. 'Why did they have to pick Edinburgh? Eh, I say? What? The shame!'

'Wrong question, Chief Inspector. The question is how do we save the Queen? Her life is more important than your disgrace,' Bell said.

'Of course, of course!' the big policeman cried. Then he turned his little eyes on the Doctor and looked helpless as a baby. 'But what can I *do*!' he moaned. 'Eh, I say? What?'

'Find the Fenians,' Joseph Bell said.

'What do they look like?' Gott wailed.

'Like you or me – young or old, probably men … but maybe females. Maybe Irish or American but could be Scots or English. You need every policeman in Edinburgh looking for clues … and I will do my best to help you – I work in the Old Town among the villains, curing their sick families, and they trust me. Not even the worst lobby sneak, burglar, coining forger, swell beggar, Lucifer dropper, turnpike sailor, child stripper or common thief wants to see Victoria harmed. They'll help me if they can. But most of all you need an awful lot of luck.'

'Child stripping?' 'What's that?' you cry. Well, I reply, a child walks down a lonely street in posh new clothes. A gang 'strips' off the clothes and sends the child home cold and crying. They sell the clothes. Cruel but common in big cities like Edinburgh at that time. If you are worried when you're out in your new clothes then try sticking them on with glue. That'll fool the child strippers!

Gott groaned.

Doctor Bell was the cleverest man in Scotland ... but even he could make mistakes. He went looking for Fenians in the poor slums of the Old Town. Maybe he should have looked in the rich houses. The sort of houses that Bairn and Bill Twist were headed for that very evening...

***

Bill Twist and Bairn passed Greyfriars Churchyard just as it was getting dark. A small, shaggy dog came to the gate of the Churchyard and wagged its tail at them.

'Hello, Bobby!' Bill Twist said and ruffled the hair on the dog's head. 'Meet my young friend, Bairn,' he said.

Bairn smiled. 'Hello, Bobby. Isn't it time you went home?'

'This is his home,' Bill Twist laughed. 'I forget, old Mr Grey didn't let you wander the streets of Edinburgh. You'll not have heard the tale of our famous Greyfriars Bobby ... the most famous dog in the world. People come from miles around just to see him!'

'He's just a dog,' Bairn shrugged.

'A very special dog ... he was owned by an old constable from the town called Jock. When Jock died they buried him and little Bobby followed his master to the graveyard. He refused to move from the grave so the local inn-keepers feed him ... and in bad weather they give him shelter.'

'He's just a dog!' Bairn cried.

Bill laughed. 'You're right, young Bairn. The rich folk of Edinburgh treat a little dog like a human hero ... then they drive back home and treat their servants like dogs.'

That was back in 1868, of course. Greyfriars Bobby chewed his last bone in 1872. There's talk of putting up a dog statue of him outside the graveyard. But let me tell you a true secret ... the people who REALLY know what happened say the stupid mongrel spent fourteen years sitting on the wrong grave!

The two crossed North Bridge and left the Old Town behind them. As Bairn's spindly legs trotted down the back lanes they dodged past the ash heaps that littered the dark alleys. The cobbled back lanes of the New Town were hidden from the fine folk who paraded in their carriages down the main streets.

Bill Twist liked the shadows where no prying police could stop him and ask what he was up to. Of course a dealer in fine china and silver always had an answer ready: 'Delivering trinkets to George Street, officer'. He just didn't want to have his name written down in a notebook. For the dodgy Twist had an even better business than being a dealer– he was a burglar.

Bairn's new master explained the plan. 'An American has moved into number 23 George Street and these Americans have more money than Queen Victoria. You will simply climb the drainpipe, drop down the chimney, fill a sack with the best stuff I've shown you around the shop ... you *know* the sort of valuables I want?'

'Yes, Master Twist.'

'And my friend says there is a silver set of knives, forks and spoons already laid out on the table. Sack them up. Climb back up the chimney, down the drainpipe and Bob's your uncle.'

'I don't have any uncles,' Bairn muttered. He wasn't happy. Dick Whittington never turned to thieving. But working in the shop was better than working up chimneys. Now he was back to chimneys ... for a while, he decided. Just for a while. 'If I'm going to be a burglar I'm going to be the best burglar in Scotland', he told himself.

So he ended up in the dark alley with bald Bill Twist. Now, sliding down dark alleys is all very well. You are hidden. But if someone decides to follow you then it is easy for *them* to hide too. And Bill Twist was being followed. A youth slipped through the shadows and watched the burglar and his boy make their way towards George Street. A youth with a hat pulled down over his head to hide his face.

Bill Twist squinted at the back doorways and made out the one for number 23. He lifted the latch carefully and crept through into the kitchen garden of the grand house.

'When you come to a branch in the chimney you pick the room that has no light showing. Take your dark lantern, pick the best ornaments and silver, then get out. Got it?'

Bairn looked up at the angel face of the shopkeeper. 'And if I get caught?'

'Don't mention my name!' Twist hissed.

'I'll hang.'

'I'll get a good lawyer to set you free … but I can't do that if I'm locked away with you. If you're caught, you're on your own.'

Bairn sighed. 'I'd better not get caught then.' He began to climb the drainpipe.

The youth in the back lane watched through a crack in the gate for a moment and set off quickly down the dark lane, kicking up clouds of cinders.

At the same time as Bairn was lowering himself into the chimney at number 23, the youth was running in through the police station door. A constable looked up from the desk where he was dealing with a drunken beggar.

'Tell Chief Inspector Gott there's a burglary taking place at number 23 George Street *now* … if he hurries he'll catch the thief!' the youth hissed.

The policeman blinked. He picked up a pencil and wrote on a piece of paper. 'Number 23 George Street … burglary in progress … now, young sir, can I have your name please?'

But the youth had melted back into the shadows of the streets. The policeman chewed his pencil. 'Chief Inspector Gott does *not* like to be disturbed.' He chewed a little more then he sighed. 'But if this is true I'll be in trouble if I don't pass on the message.'

He took the paper to the office down the corridor. He knocked and entered. Doctor Bell was seated at the table and Gott looked up angrily. 'What do you want, Constable Donald?'

'I have received information concerning a burglary...'

Gott jumped to his feet and slammed a fist on the desk. 'There is a Fenian group plotting to murder the Queen – maybe here in Edinburgh right now ... and *you* bother me with solving a burglary? How can I solve two cases at once? Eh, I say? How? Go and see the victim, Donald, take a statement and look for clues ... now get out!"

'But, sir...'

'Out! You oaf! I am on the Queen's business. Out!'

'But...' Donald said as he backed towards the door.

'One moment,' Doctor Bell said. 'I think you should let him finish ... this burglary is happening right now. You can arrest the thief *and* then get back to the Fenian plot. Isn't that right, constable?'

'Yes, sir.' Constable Donald nodded.

Gott's mouth fell open till his four chins turned to five. 'Amazing, Doctor Bell! How did you work that out? Was it the way he combed his hair? Or the dirty handkerchief hanging out of his pocket?'

Joseph Bell sighed. 'It's written on the paper in his hand ... "Number 23 George Street ... burglary in progress" … I simply read it. Now if we are really quick we may be able to catch the villain in the act.'

Gott snatched his hat and coat from the stand and his umbrella from the elephant's foot. 'Constable Donald, you should have told me as soon as you came in the room … if we lose this burglar it will be your fault.'

'Sorry, sir,' Donald said and followed the officer into the night. Gott set off for George Street.

***

At that very moment Bairn dropped into the cold fireplace of the darkened room Twist had led him to. He opened the shutter on his lantern and let the beam run quickly round the room. It was a large dining room with a long table in the centre. Silver knives, forks and spoons were laid next to snowy napkins. The boy knew that a full set of six knives, forks and spoons were worth more than the odd one.

To the side of the fireplace there was a screen. It was the sort of place the gentlemen would go when they needed the toilet in the middle of dinner.

Not that gentlemen did such a thing in Victoria's Edinburgh, of course. Not the polite ones anyway. They trotted off to the toilet. Some of them even washed their hands before they returned to chew their chops and guzzle their gravy. Some of them. The rest were plain disgusting.

Bairn turned towards the table. He paused. He heard heavy footsteps and voices outside the door.

The door handle turned and light flooded the room. A servant stepped in carrying a candleholder. Bairn just had time to dive behind the screen as the gaslights in the middle of the room flared into life.

Through the crack in the screen he watched as the servant lit the fire. It crackled into life and the servant left as three men entered.

Not only was Bairn trapped ... but his chimney escape route had been cut off too.

Bairn closed his eyes and saw the Queen's executioner and Mr Calcraft's Toilet, waiting for him.

And when Mr Calcraft sent victims dangling in his toilet he NEVER washed his hands afterwards. That's even more disgusting.

PLOTS, PRINTS AND PRISON

The three men sat at the table. One was a mountain of a man with fair hair and a checked suit. 'Gentlemen,' he said, 'be seated.' He had an American accent.

'When we speak we use our code names. I am Sunday. You ...' he went on pointing at a thin, dark, scarecrow of a man, 'are Tuesday.'

'Thank you, Mister Barton ... sorry, sir, Mister Sunday!' he replied in a Scottish accent.

The large American pointed at an old man with a tragic face. 'You are Thursday.'

'Yes, Sunday,' the man said in a soft Irish accent.

'This meeting of the Edinburgh Branch of the Fenian Brotherhood is declared open. Now, as you know, brother Michael Barratt is due to hang in four weeks' time. His only crime was to blown down a prison wall...'

'And kill twelve people, Mister Barton ... I mean Sunday,' Tuesday added.

The American shook his head. 'He did not set out to kill anyone. He got the explosive wrong. It is manslaughter. He should go to prison, maybe – but he does not deserve to die.'

'When the bomb went off in London our Michael was in Glasgow,' Thursday said. 'There were witnesses who saw him there. The court didn't believe them.'

Sunday nodded gravely. 'It is Queen Victoria who is the murderer, letting her police kill a loyal friend of ours.'

'I agree,' the old Irishman said.

'So the Fenians must strike to show we will not be bullied!' the American cried. His face was turning red. 'Victoria is evil and must be destroyed. What did she do when the Irish starved in the potato famines twenty years ago?'

'Nothing!' Thursday spat.

'She gave five pounds,' Tuesday reminded him.

Sunday sneered. 'Five pounds … when a million starved. Five pounds when two million fled to America and thousands drowned in the rotting coffin ships that went down in the Atlantic? Five pounds when the roads were black with funerals. Sure, we ate the dogs first, then the donkeys, the horses, foxes, badgers, hedgehogs and even frogs. We stewed nettles and dandelions and collected all the nuts and berries we could find. Some of us escaped to America. Five pounds and a few soup kitchens.'

The five-pound story went round Ireland like the disease that turned the potatoes black. It wasn't true. The truth was Victoria sent five THOUSAND pounds of her own money. But her enemies didn't believe that. They didn't want to believe it. So the lie stuck like mud.

'Victoria went to Ireland to see the suffering, Mr Barton ... I mean Sunday,' Tuesday said.

'And the trip cost two thousand pounds – enough to feed ten thousand starving children – just so the skinny Irish could see the fat Queen,' the leader sneered.

'I buried my wife,' the tragic Thursday muttered.

'Now I'm back from America where our brothers have raised five *hundred* pounds to help our plot. All we have to do is use the money to kill Victoria!'

Behind the screen Bairn almost gasped out loud but stuffed a sooty little hand into his mouth.

'How will we do it?' Thursday warned.

'Any way we like … but we know she comes through Waverley Station the day after tomorrow. She will stop to pick up her Scottish doctor. The famous Doctor Bell.'

'She'll be guarded,' Thursday said.

Sunday nodded. 'She'll be guarded when the train is standing at the station. So my idea is we wait till the train reaches North Bridge – a quarter mile *before* it reaches Waverley platform. It will be slowing down. We simply drop a bomb on to the roof of the royal carriage and finish her off.'

Tuesday scoffed, 'Hah! Where will we get a bomb in two days?'

Sunday smiled. He reached across the table and lifted the silver lid of a meat dish. Underneath was a black, iron ball almost as large as a schoolboy's football. Out of the top stuck a short fuse. 'This baby is packed with dynamite. Enough to blow a hole in Edinburgh Castle.'

From his hiding place behind the screen Bairn peered through a crack. He felt a chill of fear at the sight of the shining globe of death. He pushed his fist into his mouth to stop himself crying out.

Thursday gave a wintry smile. 'Revenge.'

Suddenly there was a sound like distant thunder. Someone was knocking at the front door. Sunday slammed down the cover on the meat dish to hide the bomb. Heavy footsteps rumbled along the corridor and fists thumped at the door. Sunday reached inside his long-tailed coat and pulled out a revolver. He pulled back the gun's hammer, ready to fire, then pushed it back out of sight. 'Who's there?'

'Police, sir, may we come in?'

Sunday's grip tightened on the butt of the revolver inside his jacket. 'We've been betrayed,' Tuesday said bitterly. 'They'll hang us alongside Michael Barratt!'

'I'll be proud to hang alongside my son,' Thursday said softly and rose to his feet to face the police.

'Come in,' the American called out and the door swung open.

Three men stood there. 'Good evening, sir, I am Chief Inspector Gott of the Central Police Station. Eh. I say? This is Constable Donald and a police ... erm, advisor, Doctor Bell.'

'Joseph Bell? The Queen's Doctor?' Tuesday asked.

'Yes, sir,' Doctor Bell replied, tipping his hat politely.

'How can we help you, gentlemen?' Sunday asked with a smile.

'We have received information that your house has been burgled,' Gott said sternly.

Sunday looked around. 'Most of the valuable stuff is here in this room – I don't see anything missing!'

'You haven't been in the room long, have you, sir?' Joseph Bell asked.

'How would you know that?' Sunday replied.

'The fire is burning well but the room isn't warm yet ... and there are no ashes under the grate – it's just been lit. And the candles have been burning for a quarter of an inch – you have been here for 12 or 13 minutes.'

'Amazing!' Sunday laughed. 'But what has that to do with a burglar?'

'We were told about the burglar 15 minutes ago,' Bell explained. 'If he was here 15 minutes ago ... and you got here 12 minutes ago – he didn't have time to rob the room. If he came down the chimney as I suspect ...'

'Why suspect that?' Thursday asked, his face looking tense.

'Because there have been several burglaries in the past week – I believe a new thief is loose in Edinburgh,' the Doctor explained. 'A thief who enters the houses he robs by climbing down chimneys.'

Sunday shook his large head. 'He can't be in this room. There's a fire in the grate. He must have gone into one of the other rooms. My manservant can search.'

'No,' Doctor Bell argued quietly. 'He came down the chimney, entered *this* room and didn't leave again.'

'Can you see through walls?' Sunday gasped.

The Doctor shrugged. 'No, I see the same as you. But I look more carefully. And I see a faint trail of sooty footprints leading from the fireplace...' He pointed. 'They go behind the screen ... and they don't come out again!'

'So, the thief is ...' Thursday began. Before he could finish the screen was pushed forward and fell on to the group, sending them tumbling. Bairn scrambled over the fallen screen and the writhing policemen and headed for the door. The only person in his way was Thursday. The old man pulled a wooden club from a long pocket inside his coat. Bairn ducked but the club smashed down on to the back of his head.

Why is he carrying a wooden club? Because the police carried truncheons. If this villain thought he might get into a fight with the law then he wanted it to be a fair fight. The Irish called their clubs shillelaghs and they were really just a piece of wood cut straight from a tree. Great if they got into a fight with the police from Special Branch.

Bairn's body shuddered a little and then he lay still. Chief Inspector Gott rolled out from under the wrecked screen and snapped a pair of handcuffs onto the boy's skinny wrists. 'Well done, sir,' he said to the Irishman. 'There could be a reward for this!'

THUNK!

'I don't want one!' Thursday said quickly.

The Chief Inspector frowned and shook his head in puzzlement at the old man's response. With the help of Constable Donald they carried the lifeless Bairn out of the room. Doctor Bell brushed himself down and nodded at the Fenians. 'Sorry to have disturbed your evening, gentlemen.'

'Not at all.' Sunday grinned and loosened his grip on the revolver deep in his jacket pocket to shake hands with Joseph Bell. 'We can get on with our game of cards now.'

'What cards?' the Doctor asked quietly.

'Ah … I just sent my manservant to fetch us a pack,' Sunday said smoothly. He wrapped an arm around Doctor Bell's shoulders and gently guided him towards the door. 'Good evening, Doctor … you go and make sure you take good care of your Queen!' The large American closed the door and looked at his partners. 'Because we sure plan to take care of her.'

Tuesday fretted, 'The boy must have heard our plans. We'll have to escape before he wakes up.'

Thursday snorted, 'After the crack I gave him he won't be remembering his own mother for a month. I was sorry I had to hit him so hard. He's one of us in a way … on the wrong side of the law … but I had to do it.'

'So the plan goes ahead?' Tuesday asked.

'The plan goes ahead,' Sunday said.

***

As Bairn was carried through the streets to a cell at the Central Police Station someone watched from the shadows, smiling.

'One gone. One to go.'

The youth took off his hat and marched happily down George Street towards Charlotte Square.

***

Bairn lay on a hard bench all night. He woke the next morning with a fever and a head that ached as if it had been hit by Queen Victoria's train.

A policeman brought some weak tea and a slice of bread and butter; Bairn couldn't eat anything but sipped the tea to wash away the bitter taste in his mouth. But the taste was *fear* … and all the tea in India wouldn't wash it away.

At ten o'clock the lock clanged open and Doctor Bell walked in. 'I've come to look at your head,' he said and sat Bairn on a chair. First he bathed away some blood, then he dabbed on a yellow liquid that stung but stopped the bleeding. Finally he tied on a padded bandage. 'Do you want to tell me what you were doing there, young man? Who sent you? What you've done with everything you've stolen lately?'

Bairn shook his head.

The Doctor looked at the boy with a frown. 'They could hang you. If you tell the truth they could let you go with a little hard labour then set you free.'

'They won't hang me,' Bairn said. 'He promised.'

'Who promised?'

'I don't remember. Someone. I think. I forget. I'm sure he said he wouldn't let me hang. I don't remember anything!'

That was when the guards opened the door to the cell. Rachel Mackay was standing there.

LOBSTER, LADY AND LAUGHTER

Rachel sat on the bench that Bairn had for a bed and took his hand. 'What has happened, poor boy?' she asked.

He shook his head. 'I don't know,' he whispered.

'The boy had a blow to the head and he seems to have lost his memory,' the Doctor explained

'Doctor Bell! It's wonderful to meet you – I've heard so much about you. Please tell me, do you think the poor lad will get his memory back?' Rachel asked.

'Sometimes people do – sometimes it takes a long time. But if we don't find out the truth he will hang before he ever gets his memory back!'

'Oh, no,' the girl cried. 'We can't let that happen.'

'I need to find out more about him,' Doctor Bell said as he rose to his feet and paced the small cell. 'I know he used to be a sweep boy ... not just a brush boy, but one who was sent up the chimney by the sweep. It's against the law but I know it still goes on.'

'It's cruel,' Rachel nodded. 'But how do you know that if he has no memory and can't tell you?'

The Doctor took the boy's hand from Rachel's. 'See? The skin has blackness scrubbed into it. Raise his shirt sleeve and you'll see his elbows are scarred and the scars are black. The same with his knees. You don't get that

from brushing chimneys – you get it from climbing
them.'

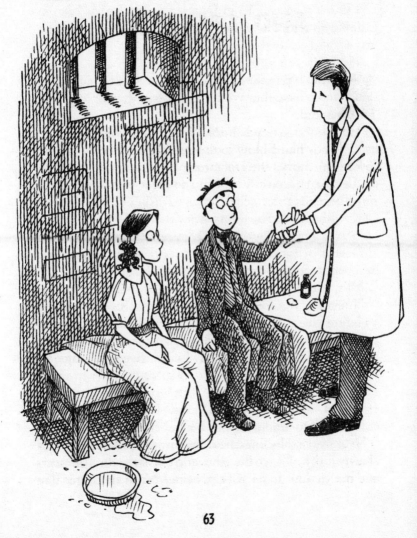

'It's true what I've heard about you! You are so clever, Doctor!' Rachel smiled.

'I know he was born in Dundee ... but he has been in Edinburgh for a few years – probably came here when he was six and ready to climb chimneys.'

'How can you know that?'

'The way he speaks. He has a faint Dundee accent but some words have more of an Edinburgh twang.'

'Amazing!'

'I think the sweep *sold* the boy to a burglar. He's been using his climbing skills to rob houses at night.'

Wrong! Rachel almost cried. As you know, *she* had rescued Bairn from the sweep and *given* him to the thief, Bill Twist. But if Rachel betrayed Bill Twist he would hang with Bairn. She didn't want that.

'Maybe the answer lies in Dundee,' Rachel said.

Doctor Bell nodded. 'This sort of boy is usually raised by a baby farmer. I can check the baby farmers of Dundee ... there can't be many of them.'

'What use would that be?' the girl asked.

'I find the name of the sweep she sold the boy to and get the name of the villain *he* sold the child on to. Then we've cracked the crime. The child's master will take all the blame and the magistrate may spare the boy's life,' the Doctor explained.

Rachel nodded. Then Doctor Bell looked at her curiously. 'Do *you* know this boy?' he asked.

'No! Not really,' she lied. 'My mother likes me to do charity work. I visit the poor and the sick, the prisoners and the victims, to see if I can help. I heard about this boy and I came to see if I could do anything. I – I saw him once when he came to sweep our chimney.'

'So you know the name of the sweep?' the Doctor asked eagerly.

She shook her head. 'The footman hired him ... and when we found he was using climbing boys we sacked the footman!'

Doctor Bell seemed to believe her. But Rachel knew that the Doctor was clever. If she said too much he would get the truth from her and she didn't want Bill Twist to suffer. She decided to say no more.

You think I'm going to tell you why? You will have to read on to find out...

The Doctor sighed. 'If I'm going to save the boy I need to be in Dundee on today's express train. But I am needed in Edinburgh. There is a plot ... so secret I can't tell you about it ... but I am helping the police seek out a gang of ruthless killers. I can't be in Dundee *and* Edinburgh.'

Rachel thought about it for a while. 'The police will be searching for the gang, I suppose ... in the wynds and tenements of the Old Town. You won't be much use searching from door to door, will you? You are better using your mighty brain to follow clues ... not searching through slums,' she said. 'Go to Dundee!'

He nodded slowly. 'I suppose you are right. I'll leave for Dundee on the noon train. Will you keep an eye on the boy? Visit him to see if he gets his memory back?'

'You can trust me,' she said softly. 'Go and do what you must do. Leave Bairn to me.'

'Who?' Dr Bell asked sharply.

'What?'

'What did you call him?'

'Er … ah … the bairn … leave the bairn to me.'

Doctor Bell rested a hand on Rachel's shoulder and squeezed it in thanks. 'Good girl.' He smiled, picked up his medical bag and left the cell.

'Oh, Bairn,' Rachel sighed. 'What are we going to do with you?'

The boy shrugged. 'Don't know, Miss Rachel.'

She turned her brown eyes on him slowly. 'You know my name?'

'Yes, Miss,' he said with a frown. 'I remember you found me in a fireplace … but I don't remember anything after that. I remember it's Kitty Bruce who's the baby farmer … but I'll not betray her to the law. And he was right about Dundee. It's just …'

'Yes?' Rachel asked quietly.

'Just … the Doctor was talking about a *plot*. I *think* I know something … something important. Something the police don't know. I *have* to remember. It's a matter of life and death.'

***

Even the express train was slow back in 1868. But Doctor Bell used the long train journey to work on the problem of the gang of killers. 'I must plot to kill the Queen,' he

66

said to himself. 'I must think like a Fenian. I can't attack her in Edinburgh because she is guarded too well – only a madman would attack in Edinburgh ...'

That's the trouble with clever people. They CAN'T always think like the rest of us. He tried to think like a Fenian – he SHOULD have been thinking like a mad Fenian! Then he'd have known they WOULD be crazy enough to attack in the city.

The train rolled on to the rail ferry that carried it over the Firth of Forth to Burntisland and Doctor Bell smiled. 'Sink the ferry! I'd sink the ferry! Wait till the Queen's train is on the ferry. Blow a hole in the side so it goes down quickly and there is no time to launch a lifeboat. The Queen dies ... along with hundreds of innocent people. But the plotters won't mind that. They didn't mind killing twelve innocent people when they blew a hole in Coldbath Fields Prison. I'd sink the ferry!'

He jumped off the train at Burntisland station and sent a telegraph message back to Chief Inspector Gott.

'Have the Queen's train diverted to bridge over Forth at Stirling. Stop. Do not use ferry. Stop. Repeat do not use ferry. Stop.'

The Doctor jumped back on the train and headed north again, happier, but with his mind still working overtime.

By evening he was in the Dundee police station asking questions and it was easy to find answers. 'Aye, if your looking for a baby farmer in these parts then Kitty Bruce is your woman. There is a warrant for her arrest here ... we want to ask her about some dead babies. Died from gin and laudanum, we think. We haven't been able to lay our hands on her. She's likely gone into hiding. You may have better luck finding her, Doctor Bell.'

Joseph Bell set off to the pitiful cottages on the riverside ... Harbour Row, the same street Ethel Scrogg had walked down 12 years before.

The house next to the Blue Bell Inn was in darkness. The front door was open. If there had ever been furniture here it had been stolen by the neighbours. Doctor Bell looked around for clues. There was nothing to say where the woman had gone.

He tapped at the window of the house next door. An ancient woman hobbled to the door and squinted up at him with half-blind eyes. 'I'm looking for Miss Bruce,' the Doctor said.

'You'll not find her here,' the old woman croaked in a voice as thin and dry as paper. 'She sold her last baby three weeks ago and moved out.'

'Do you know where she went?'

'I do. She told everyone. Said she'd heard the police had a warrant for her arrest. Something about dead babies – I'm not surprised. Some lived – some died. Babies die, don't they? Especially poor babies. But she wouldn't kill them, would she? I mean ... she got paid for every one she sold. The police haven't the brains to see that.'

'But where did she go?'

'Inverness, she said ... didn't I tell you?'

'No ... you're sure it was Inverness up north? Why

go there?'

'I didn't say she *went* there,' the old woman said with a toothless smile.

Doctor Bell nodded. 'You said Kitty Bruce *told* everyone she was going north to Inverness ... that's where she wanted the police searching?'

'You're a clever young man.'

'So she probably went south ... Glasgow or Edinburgh. She'd lose herself in the slums of either city.'

'I know she went to Edinburgh from time to time – never Glasgow. She said she had a secret there that was worth a lot of money ... a secret she'd kept for twelve long years ... those were her very words ... twelve long years. Now she was going to collect her money.'

The Doctor sighed. 'You don't know what the secret was?'

'Something about one of the children, I think she said.'

'A child?'

'A bairn,' the old woman hissed. "I'm going to collect what I'm owed for Bairn."

'A bairn?'

'No ... not *a* bairn ... for *Bairn*. Maybe she meant that poor wee boy she raised from the cradle till he was six. Kept him swaddled so he grew up small. At least he'd be sure of a job. Are you a peeler?'

'I work with the police – I help them when I can.'

'Aye, well good luck to you ... but it's Edinburgh you need to be.'

The Doctor groaned. 'I know. I know that *now*.'

He hurried back to the police station. 'Have a telegraph message sent to Edinburgh,' he told the young constable on desk duty. 'Tell the police to look out for Kitty Bruce and arrest her for child neglect if they find her.' He knew he couldn't prove she'd harmed children, but so long as she was in a cell he could ask her about the mysterious burglar boy.

The telegraph message was sent. Doctor Bell went on to the railway station to catch the night train back down south.

***

Kitty Bruce had gold in her purse. She paid for a good room in a tavern in Edinburgh's Clothmarket then went downstairs to taste the brandy they sold.

By nine o'clock that evening she was merry and buying drinks for the new friends she found in the taproom.

'I'll soon be a wealthy woman,' she boasted in her slurred voice. She showed them a sovereign. 'This is just some of the first payment … there will be hundreds more where this came from.'

'What are you selling?' a beggar woman asked, eyes glinting as brightly as the gold.

'A secret.' Kitty tapped the side of her nose and ordered another brandy.

By ten o'clock the whole bar-room was drunk on Kitty's money and singing songs of Scottish heroes. The passing police were searching for Fenians in the Old Town. They hadn't time to deal with drunks. But when someone threw a bottle out through the tavern window it landed at Constable Donald's feet. He kicked the splinters into the gutter and went in to the tavern.

Kitty Bruce was sitting on the bar, roaring a song. She stopped when she saw the constable. 'Come to arrest us, have you? Miserable lobster!'

Now calling a policeman a 'lobster' may not seem much to you. But it was a name given to the first policemen because of the helmets that had neck guards like lobster tails. The policemen hated being called that name. It spelled trouble ... and curtains for Kitty.

The room went quiet. An 'ooooh!' ran around it.

'Cobster ... pobster ... robster ... *LOBSTER*!' Kitty cried.

Constable Donald turned pink in the face – pink as lobster meat in fact. He quietly took out his handcuffs. No one spoke as he snapped them on to Kitty Bruce's wrists and dragged her off to the Central Police Station.

'Name?' the sergeant at the front desk asked.

'Kitty Bruce … not that it's any of your business,' she spat.

The sergeant picked up a telegraph message. 'If you are Kitty Bruce of Dundee then it is everything to do with me. I arrest you on the charge of child cruelty and neglect. Lock her away, Donald!'

***

The next day dawned, the way days do. Lady Mackay dressed carefully. Her maid helped her put on the make-up that hid the wrinkles on her harsh, horse-like face. She put on her hat and pulled the veil down to shade her eyes then ordered her carriage to be brought to the front door.

'Where to, My Lady?' the coachman asked.

'The magistrate's court.'

'Ah, you are on duty today, My Lady?'

'I am.' She nodded as she marched over the marble tiles of her hall and out to the carriage. 'More villains to be dealt with.' Her eyes burned so bright they seemed to give off a red glow like they were lit with the fire from Hell. 'I will sweep the streets of the human filth that dirties Edinburgh.'

'If we had more magistrates like you then we would have less crime.' The coachman chuckled as he helped her into the carriage. They clattered down George Street at a speed that had dogs and beggars, women and children scrambling out of the way.

The clerk of the court met her at the door. 'Sorry, My Lady, there are no cases today!'

'What?' she snarled. 'No one in the police cells?'

'Just a boy arrested for burglary ... but the police haven't had time to question him and ...'

'Have him brought to court!' she ordered. 'I'll ask all the questions that need to be asked ... before I send him to the gallows.'

'And a Dundee woman arrested for being drunk ... but wanted in Dundee for child cruelty.'

Lady Mackay smiled so widely she showed every one of her horse teeth. 'Oh, this is just too perfect! I will have her in my court as well.'

She went into the court room laughing like a girl.

It was not a pleasant sound.

FENIANS, FORGETTING AND FLOWERS

The clerk of the court, Mr Jeremiah Pickles, was a small man with a bald top to his head and a fringe of sandy hair – like a monk, except he had fluffy side-whiskers. Rachel sat quietly at the back of the court and watched. It was early and there were no reporters there from the press. Sometimes people enjoyed watching big trials but these little ones were like plays in an empty theatre.

The clerk stood up and read the charge. 'You are charged with the crime of burglary in that you did enter a house at 23 George Street with intent to steal. How do you plead?'

'What?' Bairn mumbled and touched the bandage on his head.

Lady Mackay leaned over the bench in front of her and her eyes burned behind the veil. 'Did you enter the house at 23 George Street?'

'That's where I was found,' Bairn agreed. 'I don't know how I got there. My memory has gone.'

'And did you enter down the chimney?'

'I was covered in soot.'

'And did you plan to steal from the house?'

'I don't remember.'

Lady Ethel Mackay gave a laugh like a bark. 'That will

74

not get you off the charge. You were in the house, you did not come through the front door … you *must have* been planning to rob it. So you are guilty, aren't you?'

'I suppose so,' Bairn agreed.

'You refused to tell the police who your master is – the man who sent you to steal and the man who would sell the goods,' Magistrate Mackay went on.

'I didn't refuse … I just don't remember.'

'A likely story. As you refused …'

'I had this crack on the head …'

'Do NOT interrupt me!' the great lady said savagely. 'Edinburgh is full of gutter filth like you. I will not sit here and set you free to rob again and again. I will not sit here and let the street-scum think they can get away with it. One burglary could get you transported to Australia. But *ten* burglaries! *TEN!* And hundreds of pounds of precious valuables gone! It deserves more than transportation. You will be taken from here to the cells at Edinburgh Castle and then you'll be taken to the Lawnmarket and you will hang by the neck till you are dead. Do you understand? I am making an example of you. Is that clear?'

Poor Bairn just shook his head, then nodded.

The clerk's bald patch caught the light from the high windows and reminded the boy of someone. Words drifted through his dark and empty memory. 'If you're caught, you're on your own,' he remembered a bald man saying.

'Take him to the cells. He may have some company before the day is through,' Lady Mackay ordered and gave a cheerless chuckle. The clerk began to lead the boy away. 'Where are you going?'

'Taking the boy to the cells, as you said, Your Worship,' the clerk answered.

'That is a job for a police officer. Why is there no policeman here today?' the magistrate snapped.

'Because the whole force is searching the Old Town, looking for some secret criminals,' he explained.

'Very well, take the boy down and bring up the woman,' the magistrate snapped and the clerk hurried to obey. Lady Mackay raised her veil and looked at the only other person in the court. Rachel. Her glowing eyes were half mad and almost frightened the girl. 'Shame. Danger. Disgrace. Ruin! But not for much longer,' Lady Ethel Mackay raged.

Rachel turned towards her and was about to speak when the door from the cells clattered open and an old woman staggered in. Her legs were weak as wet grass in a storm. She staggered as the clerk guided her to the platform with rails – the dock. Lady Mackay lowered her veil and changed her voice to a growl. 'I see the police kept you well supplied with gin and laudanum to help you sleep,' she said.

'Wha?' the woman said and tried to fix her watery eyes on the magistrate. 'Don't I know you?'

Lady Mackay pulled the brim of her hat forward so her face was shaded. 'I do not think a woman like you could possibly know a lady like me,' she snarled. 'Your name is

Kitty Bruce?'

'Aye! Pleased to meet you!' The old woman smiled a gap-toothed grin. 'Who are you?'

Lady Mackay ignored the question. 'You are charged with the murder of children in Dundee. How do you plead?'

The whiskered clerk coughed. 'No, Your Worship, the charge is child neglect and cruelty.'

The magistrate's fists went tight and for a moment it looked as though she would leave the bench and strike the little man. She took a deep breath. She spoke calmly. 'The children *died* from the cruelty and neglect. So it is murder. It's the same thing.'

'Your Worship, the punishment for neglect is transportation to the Australian colonies for seven years. The charge for murder is hanging. It is not the same thing,' Jeremiah Pickles argued bravely ... but his voice was shaking.

'Mr Pickles, the police made the charge and they made a *mistake*. I have a report here from Dundee. The police in Dundee want her charged with murder and she *shall* be.'

The little man muttered and sat down

'Don't I know you?' Kitty Bruce asked again in a slurred voice.

'You have been found guilty of murder,' Lady Mackay said in a soft-voiced rage. 'You will be taken from here and hanged by the neck until you are dead.'

'Don't I know you?' Kitty Bruce repeated.

'Take this evil woman to Edinburgh Castle and have

her hanged as soon as possible,' Lady Mackay ordered.

'But she hasn't had a trial!' Mr Pickle groaned unhappily.

'She had a trial in Dundee,' Lady Mackay said and waved a paper again as if she had read it. 'She escaped before she could hang – Dundee police are not as good as Edinburgh police. We must execute her as soon as possible – before she escapes again! Take her and the boy to Edinburgh Castle at once and hand them over to the governor for execution as soon as possible.'

'Yes, Your Worship,' the clerk said with a small bow. He led the swaying woman away.

Lady Mackay rose to her feet. 'The boy and the baby farmer will hang side by side on Calcraft's Toilet,' she snorted. 'Very neat. Very neat indeed.' She looked straight at Rachel. 'It is an example to young people today. The English writer, Mr Dickens, wants to ban hanging in public, did you know that?'

'Yes, madam.'

'Before he does you must witness these two swinging side by side. Hanging in public is a lesson for us all,' she said. Her face began to burn red like her eyes. 'Go and see it while you can. Go, girl! See what happens to villains who cross Ethel Scrogg!'

Rachel nodded silently and left the court.

***

Doctor Joseph Bell stepped wearily from the Dundee train. It's hard to sleep in a draughty carriage with clattering wheels and stinging smoke in your nose.

It's hard to sleep with your left foot in a wasps' nest too. It is never hard to sleep in a history lesson even if both feet are in a wasps' nest. Remember that next time you can't sleep.

He would just have time to take a cab to the hospital, wash and shave, then go to the Central Police Station to see how the search for the Fenians was going.

The ticket collector grinned. 'Good morning, Doctor Bell. What can you tell me this morning? You always know something amazing about people!' The man in the black uniform turned to a young lady waiting to catch a train. 'Amazing man is the Doctor! You'll see.'

Joseph Bell sighed, tired and red-eyed. 'You had porridge for your breakfast and when you fed it to your baby, the baby was sick. You really should feed it better, Cameron.'

The ticket collector grinned wider. 'See? What did I tell you?' He laughed as he clipped the Doctor's ticket and waved him through the barrier. 'Amazing!'

The young woman shook her head. 'Not really – you have porridge on your tie and baby vomit on your shoulder. Ticket to Falkirk, please.'

***

As Doctor Bell's cab headed out of Waverley Station he passed a police wagon. He didn't know that it was the very police wagon carrying Bairn and Kitty Bruce to Edinburgh Castle. Rachel sat with them in the wagon that had only a tiny, barred window in the roof to let in light.

The baby farmer snored, still drugged with gin and laudanum. But Bairn was as bright as ever. 'Don't worry about the hanging, Bairn,' Rachel said. 'It won't hurt.'

Bairn shook his head. 'It won't hurt because I won't hang!' He laughed. 'Miss Bruce says if you're born to hang, you'll hang. If you're not born to hang, you won't. And I wasn't. I was born to live a long and happy life. I remember her saying that. I'll be the greatest man in Scotland. This is just a little setback.'

Rachel could see the sad boy believed it. She tried to explain what would happen. 'In the old days they used to send you up a ladder with a rope round your neck and twist it till you fell off. Now they place you on a trapdoor, pull the bolts to open the trap and let you drop. It's much quicker. You won't feel a thing.'

'What did you say?' he asked and rubbed his head.

'I said you won't feel a thing.'

'Before that,' he said. 'About the ladder?'

'I said they turn you off. That's what they call it – turning you off ... but they don't do that now.'

'You didn't say "turn" ... you said "twist" ... that's it. Twist! I remember now. The bald man. Twist! He was my master. Bill Twist. He was the one who said he'd make sure I didn't hang. He has a shop in the High Street ... I work for him!'

Rachel nodded. 'I know, Bairn. I got you the job. But he's an honest dealer in trinkets. My family have known him for years.'

Bairn laughed and pulled off the bandage. 'No! He steals them … he sends them to Glasgow to be sold – and a burglar friend of his in Glasgow sends loot from over *there* to be sold *here*. It must have been Mr Twist that sent me down the chimney … I'm sure. And he will get me a lawyer to set me free … he promised.'

'Bairn,' Rachel said gently. 'It's too late for lawyers. You've *had* your trial.'

He frowned. 'But can't you have a second trial?'

'An appeal?' the girl said.

'Yes! If Mr Twist comes forward with his lawyers they will get me off,' Bairn argued. 'I wasn't born to hang, Rachel. I wasn't born to hang!'

'Very well. When they take you into Edinburgh Castle I'll go back into the town and seek out Mr Twist. I'll see what I can do.'

The girl took the laudanum bottle out of Kitty Bruce's bag but left her with the gin. 'If we take her sleeping drug away she may remember things better. She may remember everything is her fault. And that could save you from the rope. You do remember this is your Aunt Kitty, don't you?' the girl asked.

A slow smile spread across Bairn's face. 'Yes,' he nodded. 'Yes, that's coming back to me. She brought me up. Looked after me. Now it's my turn to look after her.'

Rachel nodded as she put the laudanum in her pocket.

In the gloomy wagon Bairn's pale face glowed. 'You're a real friend, Miss Rachel. A real friend! I won't forget you.' No – he definitely wouldn't forget her…

***

When Mr Pickles, the Clerk of the Court, opened the back door of the prison van Rachel climbed down into the bright morning air. Edinburgh Castle courtyard was full of filthy, crushed souls being marched to the cells by weary policemen. It seemed half of the Old Town was under arrest.

Guards in bright, brass-buttoned uniforms led Bairn into the cells and carried the snoring Kitty Bruce. Bairn gave the girl a final wave and smile.

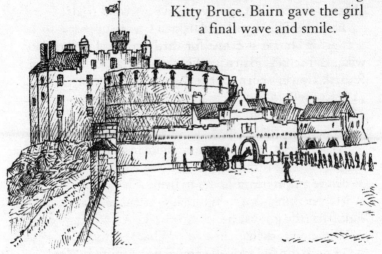

'When do they hang?' she asked Mr Pickle.

'Tomorrow morning at eight,' he said. 'Twenty-two hours' time.' The man pulled out a handkerchief and mopped his bald patch. 'I suppose the old woman deserves to die ... but the boy. Ah, if only something could be done to save the boy! Such a waste of a young life. And Lady Mackay was so...'

'So what?' Rachel snapped.

He looked at Rachel, nervously. 'Nothing, Miss. Nothing.'

She turned towards the morning sun and marched down the huge Castle courtyard and the High Street. 'Let's go and see Bill Twist, shall we?' she said to herself.

Policemen were everywhere, knocking on tenement doors in the shadowed wynds where the sun never shone.

Their search for a Fenian gang was supposed to be secret. Of course a secret like that can never be kept for long. But secrets get twisted in the telling.

The flower-seller at the Mercat Cross told Rachel, 'They're looking for Fenians! They say there's a plan to blow up Edinburgh when the Queen gets here!'

'What?' Rachel gasped. 'The whole of Edinburgh?'

'Yes! There are a hundred Fenians in the city and they'll set off a hundred bombs tomorrow at ten o'clock. We have twenty-four hours to live!'

'If you think that why don't you run off to Leith or Falkirk?' the girl asked.

The flower-seller sneered, 'What? And have some villain rob my house while I'm gone? I think not!'

It was madness. But Rachel thought it would be wise to take a carriage ride out of Edinburgh tomorrow morning … just in case … after she'd seen Kitty Bruce and Bairn hang, side by side of course.

CONSTABLE, CASTLE AND COBBLES

'**W**hat have you found?' Doctor Bell asked Chief Inspector Gott. A strong cup of tea was keeping him awake.

'Nothing,' the policeman sighed. 'We have searched every house and every hovel in the Old Town. We have found more stolen gold than there is in the Bank of Scotland ... we have found enough thieves to fill Edinburgh Castle five times over. But not a sign of a bomb anywhere. And no sign of this Kitty Bruce you were looking for.'

The Doctor nodded. 'So the Fenians are outside of Edinburgh ... or living in the New Town.'

'And we can't search there! Eh, I say? What?' Gott groaned. 'The rich folk will just refuse to let us in! We'll need a thousand search warrants ... and the magistrates won't sign warrants to search their friends' homes! No, if the Fenians are hiding in the New Town they are very rich ... and rather clever!'

'They have American money so they're rich enough,' Doctor Bell said.

Gott scratched his head. 'I've met an American in the past week,' he said. 'I just can't remember where. Eh, I say? Where? And when...?'

The Doctor yawned. 'I'm sorry, Chief Inspector. I am exhausted by that wasted trip to Dundee. I need some sleep then I'll be able to help you. And the boy burglar case will have to wait too.'

There was a distant boom that shook the windows of the Chief Inspector's room. 'The one o'clock cannon from the Castle,' he sighed. 'But it'll be another sort of boom if we don't find the Fenians before tomorrow morning. Twenty-one hours, Doctor. Twenty-one hours.'

***

The Doctor returned to his lodgings and slept the afternoon away.

In the Central Police Station Constable Donald knocked on the Chief Inspector's door. 'Sir, I've just come on duty and seen we're looking for a baby farmer called Kitty Bruce.'

'Are we?'

'There was a telegraph message from the Dundee police?'

'Ah! Doctor Bell's case. He went to Dundee to find the woman but it seems she's run off. We can't be looking for her while we're looking for the Fenians.'

'No, sir,' Donald said and his mean mouth looked smug. 'But I arrested her last night for being drunk!'

Gott raised an eyebrow. 'Doctor Bell will be pleased.'

'Shall I tell him she's in the cells?'

'No, let him sleep. She'll keep. She isn't important.'

But when Donald went to check he found Kitty Bruce wasn't in the police cells. She had been taken to court that morning and not returned. Maybe she'd gone free with a fine, he thought.

He shrugged. 'She's not important,' the Chief Inspector had said. Constable Donald went back on the streets of Edinburgh to track down beggars and thieves and search for Fenians.

But there weren't any to be seen.

'Where are all your villain friends today?' Constable Donald asked the flower-seller at the Mercat Cross.

She spat on the cobbles. '*Your* friends have arrested them all. The Castle is bursting with them. They're packing them in the cells. Beggars are sleeping on the floors and the thieves are sleeping on the beggars! Never mind ... they'll all go free when the Fenians blow up Edinburgh tomorrow ... eighteen hours from now.'

You can go to the Mercat Cross today and NOT see ancient spit on the cobbles. This is because the ancient rains of Edinburgh have washed them away. But this does NOT mean it's all right for YOU to spit on Edinburgh's streets. An old lady could slip on your spit and hurt herself. Don't do it!

Sunday sat by the fireplace with pieces of fuse. 'I light the fuse,' he said.

'Go!' said Thursday in his lilting Irish voice.

Tuesday held the fuse that Sunday passed to him. He counted the seconds, 'One …two … ouch!' he cried as the fuse burned down to his fingers. He sucked them. 'You burned me.'

The big American sighed. 'You should have dropped it.'

'It hurts!'

'Not as much as hanging will hurt Michael Barratt,' Sunday said.

The Irishman, Thursday, gave a moan of pain. 'Sorry,' Sunday said softly. 'Michael … he's your son … I sometimes forget.'

Thursday set his jaw tight. 'Revenge.'

'Revenge,' Barton agreed.

'My fingers hurt,' Tuesday complained.

'Two inches of fuse is two seconds … four inches is four seconds. We need three inches … three seconds. Let's try again,' Sunday said.

He lit the fuse. 'One … two … three …'

'Ouch! I'll have no fingers left at this rate,' Tuesday cried.

'The main thing is Queen Victoria will have no *head* left tomorrow,' Thursday told him. He stood up, raised the silver dish cover and took out the black bomb. 'I would like the honour of dropping this, Sunday, sir,' the American said.

Sunday nodded slowly. 'That leaves me free, with the gun, in case there are any problems. I keep watch on North Bridge. Thursday, you hold the bomb over the side as soon as the train gets close. Tuesday ... you light the fuse when the locomotive passes under the bridge. Thursday, count to two and drop the bomb. On the count of three it will explode just as the Queen's carriage passes underneath.'

And us?' Tuesday asked. 'The blast could kill us too.'

'Not if you drop it and duck behind the wall ... you will live to fight another day, brother Tuesday. Till tomorrow at ten o'clock,' he said.

Then he walked over to the piano, lifted the lid and cried, 'Gentlemen ... the anthem!'

He crashed out a tune and the three men sang in a tuneless roar.'

'God save Ireland!' said the heroes;
'God save Ireland' said they all.
Whether on the scaffold high
Or the battlefield we die,
Oh, what matter when for Ireland dear we fall!

 The song was written in 1867. When the three Manchester Fenians were hanged, the song became the Fenian anthem.

***

Chief Inspector Gott's chins were shaking. He pushed his fat form along the corridor of the Central Police Station; he pushed past the stinking humans who were packed in. 'Where have all these villains come from?' he roared.

It was hard being heard over the noise of men, women and children who were bawling things like, 'I'm innocent!

I shouldn't be here! I never saw that stolen candlestick in my life and if I did I didn't steal it. Who's going to feed the cat if you lock me away? You have the wrong man! If I robbed a bank I wouldn't be standing here with holes in me shoes! Let me go and I'll tell you it was my mother that stole the old man's umbrella!'

Constable Donald shouted over their heads, 'Sorry, sir, the cells are full. I went out to arrest more but they've all been arrested.'

'So take this lot to the Castle!'

'Sorry, Chief Inspector, but the Castle's full too! Our lads have arrested so many on suspicion we have every rogue in Edinburgh locked up,' the constable explained.

'Take their names, write a report and set them free … we'll deal with them after we find the Fenians,' Gott grumbled and finally pushed through to the constable's side. 'And empty the Castle cells too … it must be costing a fortune to feed this lot. I want every man looking for the assassins.'

'Yes, sir,' the constable said and stumbled over thieves, beggars and cheats to get to the door. He tried to get the crowd into a line to take names. But most gave false names – there were three Queen Victorias and four Greyfriars Bobbies. But most just pushed past him to freedom. In minutes the corridors were empty except for the sewer smell that lingered behind. The streets of Edinburgh were once again half-full of the greatest criminal brains in the city.

The other half was in the Castle. Constable Donald set off to North Bridge and at World's End he turned into the High Street. He began to climb the hill to the Castle and passed the gallows being hammered together outside the church of St Giles. Someone was due to hang in the morning, he guessed.

This was the spot where Deacon Brodie had hanged – the famous Brodie, a church minister by day and a burglar by night. And it was on the same courtyard that the Earl of Montrose had been butchered two hundred years before.

He was taken through the streets to the Mercat Cross. He had to climb a ladder, tall as a house so everyone could see him, and a rope was placed round his neck.

The ladder was taken away and he was left to swing for 3 hours. Then the Earl was cut down and his body carved up. His head was stuck on Edinburgh Tollbooth (where people coming into Edinburgh would see it).

His arms and legs were sent to Glasgow, Stirling, Perth and Aberdeen to be put on show. His body was buried in a common grave – they say his wife dug it up and had the heart cut out. It was sent to his son in Holland.

Constable Donald knew what would happen to the Fenian assassins if they were caught, they'd be chopped into pieces and never put back together. He was sweating as he plodded up the steep slope to the Castle and worried that he was getting Mr Gott's orders right. Mr Gott could be a harsh boss at times and he had a few cruel punishments for constables who let him down … night patrol in the

Grassmarket was dark and dangerous and no one wanted to do it. Or being a beggar-hunter … wearing ordinary clothes and catching poor people who tried to beg for food or money.

Donald shuddered. He walked among street-sellers and beggars, the maids out shopping and the delivery boys idling against walls. He was too distracted to notice that he was being followed by a youth. The youth had a broad hat with a wide brim that hid his face. But even under the shadow of the brim the youth could be seen looking up at the gallows and smiling.

Constable Donald walked through the gate of the Castle and the youth turned away and walked back down the hill towards The Mound Road that led down from the Castle, over the gardens and back to Princes Street.

Constable Donald crossed the Castle courtyard over the cobbles. There were still dark patches in from where they'd burned witches till a hundred years ago. Men and women had been tied to a stake on top of a pile of wood. If they were lucky the executioner would strangle them quickly before he lit the fire. If they were unlucky they would die slowly and painfully in the fire. The policeman was all in favour of hanging … but burning seemed too cruel even for him.

He nodded to the guard. 'Good morning. I've come to set your prisoners free.'

The guard squinted at the policeman. 'What? All of them?'

'That's what Chief Inspector Gott says.'

The guard leaned on his rifle. 'To tell the truth the

smell and the shouting is so bad I'll be glad to be rid of them.'

Donald nodded. 'It was the same in the Central Police Station. It's these Fenians that's making all the trouble.'

'What Fenians?'

'I'm not allowed to say. It's a secret. I can't tell you about the plot to assassinate Victoria tomorrow morning,' Donald said.

'I've heard about it!' the guard cried. 'So it's true!'

'I'm not allowed to say,' Donald said sternly.

'Course not! Course not! Mum's the word,' the guard said with a wink. 'Right, I'll just get the captain of the guard and set these wretches free. Be glad to be rid of them.'

'So you said.'

Bairn sat in the upright cell. Kitty Bruce was still snoring in the corner but the other prisoners were sitting on the floor and on the sleeping bench listening to the boy.

Some people are born to hang ... and that's not me!'

'You'll hang in the morning along with the baby

farmer,' a young pickpocket girl called Izzie said. When the police had searched her house, looking for Fenians, they found a gold watch that a gentleman had lost the day before. She hadn't had time to sell it.

'No,' Bairn grinned. 'I'll go free. You just wait and see.'

And no sooner had he said it than a guard in a uniform with bright silver buttons clattered his keys in the door. It creaked open. Fourteen pairs of frightened eyes ... and one pair of shining Bairn eyes ... looked up at him. 'You're all free to go!' the guard said.

The villains scrambled to their feet and rushed for the door – they feared someone would decide it was a mistake. Only Bairn hung back with the pickpocket girl. 'Amazing! You should burn as a witch,' she told him. 'You *said* you'd go free and you *did*!'

Bairn looked at Kitty Bruce. 'But I can't leave my aunt Kitty behind,' he said.

Izzie squeaked. 'But she told us she *sold* you to a sweep after she drugged you and starved you for years. You might not remember how you got here but you remember when you were a tiny boy. She's evil. Leave her, Bairn. Escape while you can.'

'No,' he said. 'I'll stay till she wakes up. We'll leave together.'

'Once the Fenian attack is over the police might remember you. They'll remember you weren't supposed to be set free. You aren't like the rest of us – we were just being held till we answer questions. *You're* being held till you hang!'

'I wasn't born to hang,' Bairn said, stubborn as ever.

'Maybe not. If anyone can escape from here, it's you,' she said.

'How?' Bairn asked.

'It's been done before,' Izzie called as she gathered her shawl and purse. 'One moonless night in 1314 Thomas Randolf carried out one of the most amazing raids in history – ever. Randolf and thirty of his men captured the Castle. The English had taken the place and Randolf wanted to get it back for the Scots.'

'Did he have cannon to blast the walls?' Bairn asked.

Izzie shook her head. 'No, he climbed the north cliff below the Castle – just outside this cell. When they got to the top of the cliff they put ladders against the wall. Randolf led the way over and the Scots massacred the defenders. The Castle cobbles were a river of blood, they say.'

'Nice,' Bairn muttered.

'It seems Randolf met an old man called William Frank who had been a Castle guard many years before. Frank had a girlfriend who lived down here in the town and he liked to sneak out to see her.

'He knew a path down the cliff and he showed it to Randolf. They made ladders to climb those walls at the top – they're not high walls there because the defenders think the cliffs below make them safe!'

'Serves the English right,' Bairn said. 'They should have had guards there anyway.'

'But they did! In fact one English guard looked over the wall just as they reached the top of the cliff. He shouted out, "I can see you!" and threw down a rock. But it seems the guard was just having a laugh – trying to frighten his mates inside – and had seen nothing. Once the Scots were in they murdered the guards on the wall and cut the throats of the soldiers still in their beds. Some of the defenders jumped off the walls to escape the Scottish swords.'

'That must have made a mess on King's Stables Road,' Bairn snorted.

Izzie moved towards the open door. 'In the old days toilets were just a hole in the wall – the human waste was just left to drop down and stain the wall. Now they have a pipe to carry it away into a sewer at the bottom,' she told him.

'Why do I want to know that?' Bairn asked.

'I'm telling you a way that a clever climbing boy like you could escape from the Castle if he can get out on to the wall,' she explained. 'I don't want to see you die!'

'Thanks,' Bairn said.

Izzie gave him a quick kiss on the cheek then hurried out. The guard looked at Bairn. 'Aren't you leaving too?'

The boy shook his head nodding towards the old woman snoring on the floor behind him.

'I'll have to lock you both in then,' the man said and turned the key.

Bairn wandered over to the bench and sat on it holding his aching head. 'Fenian attack?' he muttered. 'Fenian attack? I *know* something about that … I know *all* about it … I'm sure. I just … just can't remember!'

CASTLE, CLIMBERS AND CUT-THROATS

Doctor Bell lived at the western end of Princes Street – just on the corner of Lothian Road.

Rachel ran up the stairs to his apartment and knocked on his door. An old housekeeper answered and peered through her spectacles at the young girl. 'Can I help?'

'I need to see Doctor Bell. Is he at home?'

'He's just woken up. He was travelling all night and he needed a nap.'

'But I can see him?'

'I'll ask,' she said and closed the door in the girl's face. A minute later she returned and let her in. The Doctor's rooms were gloomy with heavy old furniture and thick curtains. There was the smell of tobacco smoke and a fog in the air.

The Doctor was sitting in a high-backed chair with a pipe and staring into a log fire that gave a warmer glow to the room.

'Rachel!' he said looking up. He spoke to his housekeeper, 'Mrs Wilson, please bring us a pot of tea.' Then he leaned forward and looked at Rachel. 'How are you?'

'What did you find in Dundee?' she asked urgently. 'Anything that could help the bairn?'

The Doctor sucked hard on his pipe stem and blew out

a thick haze of smoke. 'The wicked Miss Bruce left three weeks ago with a "secret" her old neighbour said. A secret worth some money. That can only mean one thing ... blackmail! Kitty Bruce knows something about someone. I'd guess she's in Edinburgh and she will want to be paid to keep quiet.'

Rachel nodded. 'It must be an important person,' she said.

'I sent a telegraph from Dundee telling the Edinburgh police to look out for her,' the Doctor said.

Rachel smiled. 'And they found her,' she said. 'She will hang in the morning!'

Doctor Bell looked suddenly ill and fell back into his chair. 'Hang?! Oh, no! She was never meant to hang! That can't be right. She was only charged with cruelty.'

At that moment the door opened and Mrs Wilson brought in the tea. She placed the tray on the table between them and raised the teapot. 'I'll pour the tea,' Rachel told her. The old servant sniffed and left the room.

'I can't see a woman hang because of a mistake,' the Doctor groaned.

'A mistake?'

'The Dundee police said cruelty ... not murder! Somehow the message has been muddled. I'll have to see if I can stop the execution!'

'You're very tired,' Rachel said. 'You need a cup of tea before you go racing all over Edinburgh. Let me pour you a cup,' she offered and pulled the pot towards her. Doctor Bell closed his eyes and began thinking hard. He didn't see the girl take Kitty's bottle of laudanum from her pocket and stir a large spoonful into his cup of tea.

What a thoughtful girl. If you were tired wouldn't you like a kind friend to drug you into a restful sleep without telling you? No? Then you're not much of a friend is all I can say.

'Kitty Bruce has ruined too many lives, Doctor,' Rachel said softly. 'It would be wrong to save her worthless life. You're tired,' she said. 'Rest a while longer.'

I'm sorry if you think this was a wicked thing to do. Sometimes people do terrible things to make other things happen. Good things. Well ... good for THEM anyway. Doping a doctor is not so very bad, is it? I mean, doctors dope people all the time before they operate and nobody says THAT is wicked, do they?

Doctor Bell raised the cup to his lips and was about to drink when there was a soft tap on the door. 'Enter!' he called. Mrs Wilson came in with some scones on a tray and the evening newspaper.

The Doctor placed the newspaper on his lap and raised the teacup to his lips again. Then something caught his eye. He lowered the teacup and picked up the paper. The front page was covered in news of police arrests. The reporter had guessed the police were looking for Fenians and the public were told to be on their guard when Queen Victoria arrived tomorrow. The newspaper was offering a £100 reward if a reader could tell the police where to find the assassins.

So much for the 'secret' search.

But the Doctor ignored the main news. A small article at the bottom of the page said, '*Baby farmer to hang.*' He pointed to it excitedly. 'See this?'

Dundee woman, Kitty Bruce, has been found guilty of child murder. She was arrested last night, taken to court this morning and will hang tomorrow outside St Giles along with a boy thief. The boy is believed to be the burglar who has robbed at least ten houses in the New Town in the past two weeks by climbing down chimneys. A large crowd is expected for the hanging – the first in Edinburgh for four years. Some say public hanging will be banned soon. This may be the last time Scots get to see a hanging. Up to 20,000 people are expected as the entertainment at the gallows will be followed by the chance to see Queen Victoria pass though Waverley Station in her train.

Doctor Bell put the paper down, rose to his feet and looked at Rachel. He still hadn't touched his tea. 'It's all wrong. I was in Dundee yesterday – they said nothing about murder. And I fear the boy burglar may be your little friend. I need to find out what has happened. We need to move quickly,' the Doctor said urgently.

'As soon as you finish your tea,' Rachel said kindly, trying to slow the Doctor down.

'Never mind about that. I feel fresh again after that nap earlier. Let's go now.'

'Let's'. The girl sighed and followed him out of the house into the busy afternoon streets.

They hurried down Lothian Street and into King's Stables Road. Rachel realized they were not going the quickest way to the Castle. If Doctor Bell wanted to save Kitty Bruce and Bairn then he was going a long way round. 'Why are we going this way?' she asked.

'Because I can't save either of them if I don't have the facts,' he said.

'But this is the way to the dirtiest slums in the city,' Rachel said as they reached Grassmarket.

'This is where I do most of my work,' Doctor Bell told her. 'The poor can't afford doctors so I come here to do what I can. They seem to like me and they're the ones to help us.'

Rachel wrinkled her nose at the animal smells of Grassmarket … the market where animals were traded … and they walked up to the Last Drop Inn. The Doctor turned and entered. Rachel followed.

It's called the Last Drop because the market here used to be a popular place for hanging people – they drop with a rope round their necks and it's their last drop.

Several men and women greeted the Doctor as he entered the gloomy room. There was sawdust on the floor to soak up the spilled ale and drunks' vomit and the dog pooh. Most landlords would change the sawdust when it got dirty – the landlord of the Last Drop Inn just seemed to scatter more sawdust on top of the filth.

The Doctor grinned at the greasy man behind the bar. 'Hamish, I want my chimney swept.'

'I'm a landlord! What do you want me to do? Climb on your roof and pour a barrel of ale down to clean it?'

Doctor Bell laughed. 'No, my friend, but I'll bet *you* know the name and address of a good sweep who can help me.'

The landlord wiped his greasy hands on a greasier cloth and shrugged. 'I know half a dozen.'

'Ah,' the Doctor said in a low voice. 'But I don't want just *any* sweep. I want one that will send a climbing boy up the chimney.'

'Doctor! You shock me! That is against the law … as you know,' the man behind the bar said trying to look shocked.

'Selling smuggled whisky is against the law, my friend, but it doesn't stop *you* from doing it. I won't tell the law about your whisky and you won't tell the law about me wanting a climbing boy.'

'Aye, Doctor, you're a terrible man.' The landlord sighed. 'Let's say I did *not* tell you the man you want is Georgio Grey. And I didn't tell you he lives in Chambers Street at the South Bridge end.'

Doctor Bell threw a shilling on the bar and said, 'Have yourself a drink,' then turned and walked out of the filthy bar into the filthier street.

Rachel was half-running to keep up with him. 'Why are we looking for a sweep?' she asked.

'The boy, Bairn, was a sweep. Like I said before, the soot in his skin shows he was a climbing boy for a few good years. His master should lead us to the burglar. I went to Dundee to track him down the legal way. Now there's no time – I have to use my criminal contacts.'

Rachel trotted alongside him past Greyfriars Church. The little dog, Bobby, was being fed by visitors. Sweet.

'Grim place,' Doctor Bell said. 'Two hundred years ago some rebels lost a battle at Bothwell Bridge ... and paid dearly for it. The King had them kept for five months without shelter in a corner of Greyfriars' Churchyard. Their only food was a penny loaf every day and each man got a handful of water. If they tried to get up to escape during the night the guards would shoot them. At the end of five months the remaining rebels were sent to the West Indies to work as slaves but the ship was wrecked near the Orkney Islands and only forty survived. Kings can be cruel.'

'And Victoria? If she's cruel why are you trying to save her?'

'If the people turn against Victoria they can send her home to Germany where her family came from – no need to *kill* people to get what you want. I want Victoria to live ... I want Bairn to live. Hah!' He laughed. 'I even want Kitty Bruce to live – so long as she can never harm an innocent child again. Now, here we are, Chambers Street. Let's see what Master Sweep Grey has to say for himself, shall we?'

'No, wait!' Rachel said sharply. 'He will not take you seriously if you have a girl with you. I'll go to the shops in South Bridge while you talk to him.'

Yes, dear reader YOU know that Rachel rescued Bairn from Mr Grey. YOU know that Mr Grey would tell Doctor Bell, 'THAT'S the girl that made me give up Bairn. If you want to know who Bairn was passed on to then ask HER!' And that would never do, would it? She is a shifty young lady, this Rachel. It would pay you to keep an eye on her.

BLACK BULL AND BILL

Have you ever seen a puppet show? The puppets dance on strings. That was how Doctor Bell walked but he was even jerkier when he was excited.

He strode away from Mr Grey's house and Rachel followed.

'High Street ... Twist!' Doctor Bell said simply.

'Twist?'

'Mr Bill Twist.'

'Doesn't he keep a shop for silver and china trinkets?' Rachel asked. They crossed South Bridge and the girl was trotting to keep up with the man striding ahead of her. She was afraid Bill Twist had been betrayed and her effort to save him had misfired like an old musket.

> Muskets could explode and blow up in the face of the person firing them. If they were lucky they just lost a few fingers. At one time in the 1600s the Army used to bury more fingers than men!

'What did the sweep Mr Grey say?'

'He finally told me that he'd bought a boy called Bairn from Kitty Bruce – she'd brought him up to be a climbing boy – small and thin. He had to pay top price for him.

Then he said a youth came to him one evening with a message for him to clean a chimney, with a climbing boy, in the New Town. When he sent Bairn up the chimney a girl in the house threatened to report Mr Grey to the police. He had to give up Bairn to save his own skin.'

'I see ... and does he know which house?' Rachel asked.

'No, the youth that delivered the message told him to read the address then destroy it ... which he did. Now he can't remember ... somewhere at the western end of the New Town, he thinks.'

'So who was the youth?'

'I don't know ... he was wearing a hat with a wide brim that hid his face. Mr Grey didn't take much notice.'

'Ah,' she nodded. 'So why are we going to see Bill Twist?'

'Mr Grey says he didn't know what the girl did with Bairn. But he was walking up High Street last week and he saw Bairn coming out of Twist's shop ... the boy was carrying some wrapped parcels.'

'He'd bought some china?' Rachel suggested.

'No ... boys like that don't buy china. He must have been *delivering* the china – or silver or ornaments. Bill Twist must be his new master!'

'No, no!' Rachel argued. 'You can't be sure!'

'It's the only clue I have,' the Doctor said and hurried on.

They turned right into High Street and down the hill towards Holyrood Palace.

The Palace where King James VI put Agnes Sampson on trial for being a witch. He said she tried to sink royal ships by throwing live cats into the sea at Leith with a dead man's bones and joints tied to them.

Agnes was tortured with a Witch's Bridle. She was pinned to a wall of her cell by an iron mask that had four sharp prongs. These were forced into her mouth, against her tongue and cheeks.

Then she was 'thawed' – a rope was wrapped around her head and twisted till it became tighter and tighter, crushing her skull. Then she was kept without sleep for several days till she said she was guilty. Finally she was taken up this hill to the Castle to be strangled and burned.

Bill Twist's shop was halfway down the High Street on the right. It faced north, which was handy because the sun didn't shine into the window to fade the paintings. 'I'll wait out here,' Rachel said.

She wandered down the street to look in the shop windows while Doctor Bell was inside talking to Bill Twist. She spotted a fine silver necklace that would look good around her neck. Father could buy that for her, if she asked him, she thought. It was growing dark now and gaslights were going on in the shop windows. The street gaslamps made the place a little safer. But the gas factories down in Canongate gave off their filthy stench.

At last Doctor Bell came out of Bill Twist's shop. Rachel stood in a shop doorway so that Twist couldn't see her. The shopkeeper looked miserable and defeated as he scuttled back into his shop and locked the door.

The girl stepped out into the High Street.

'As I thought,' the Doctor said. 'Twist bought Bairn from some girl. By day he was a delivery boy ... by night he was a chimney-climbing thief.'

Did I mention Rachel took money for Bairn? Probably not. You may call her a slave trader if you like – selling the boy. But she had rescued him and sent him to a better life so why shouldn't she take a small reward to buy herself a new dress? That's what you would do if you managed to sell off your horrible little brother, isn't it?

'The girl? Who is she?'

'Twist refuses to name her.' Doctor Bell sighed. 'Some

wicked young lady from the New Town. If Twist won't talk and Bairn can't remember we may never know.'

Rachel smiled secretly in the shadow of the gas lamp as they walked back up the hill towards the Castle.

'I won't have Twist arrested … not yet. I've too much to do. Fifteen hours' time and Victoria arrives and I still haven't found this nest of assassins. But I've warned Twist that if there are ever any chimney thefts in Edinburgh again I will send Chief Inspector Gott straight round to his shop.'

Rachel nodded. 'And now you'll carry on with the search for the Fenians?'

The Doctor stopped suddenly. 'I need to save the boy's life and I have one mystery left to solve before I can do that.'

'What?' Rachel asked.

Doctor Bell's eyes glittered in the green glow of the gas lamps. 'Bairn was *not* discovered by the police. He was betrayed. He was sent to 23 George Street so he could be caught!'

'No!' Rachel gasped. 'Why on earth would anyone want a sweep boy caught?'

'Because Bairn has a secret. A secret dangerous to someone. So dangerous they want him executed. They want the secret to die with him,' Doctor Bell explained.

'How do you *know*?' the girl asked.

'Bill Twist told me something important – something so useful I let him go free, for the time being anyway. He told me that he was tipped off that 23 George Street was a good place to rob. A youth in a wide-brimmed hat brought the message. And I think that same youth appeared in the police station to report that Bairn was busy robbing 23 George Street,' the Doctor added. 'The youth set up the robbery in George Street, probably followed Twist and the boy to the house, then betrayed them to the police.'

Rachel gave a shudder of the sort she had seen ladies give in a drama on the stage.

You can try this next time you tell a whopping great lie. That's if you don't mind looking like an actress on a stage.

'Oh! But while you were in Twist's shop ... I'd swear there was a youth like that at the corner of World's End!'

'Doing what?'

'Nothing – just watching Twist's shop while you were in there ... and he disappeared when you came out!' she cried.

'Did you get a good look at him?'

'Ohhhh!' Rachel groaned. 'I didn't think it was important. He had the broad hat, as you say – a brown felt hat. And a dark green coat with black breeches.'

'His face? Did you see his face?'

Rachel closed her eyes and tried to picture the messenger at the corner. 'It was in shadow, of course ... but just then the old lamplighter came round and turned on the lamp outside the shop ... just for a moment the youth looked up and I caught a glimpse of his face. A cruel, cruel face. It made me shiver.'

'Good, Rachel. But what was so cruel about it?'

She clapped her hands suddenly. 'The mouth! His mouth was twisted – twisted up … but only at one corner … as if he had a scar. A cruel, scarred face.'

'A scar on which side?'

'The … the left, it must have been.'

Doctor Bell started walking his jerky walk on the spot. 'Brilliant – one day you'll be a detective like me! This youth should be easy to find. Someone *must* know him – and who his master is.'

He walked up the hill towards the Castle. 'Aren't you going to ask your villain friends in the Grassmarket about him?' Rachel asked.

'No time. It could take hours and I don't have hours. Bairn will hang in the morning. No, I'll ask the two people who might *know* who wants to see Bairn and Kitty Bruce dead … I'll ask Bairn and Kitty themselves!'

'They're in prison in the Castle,' Rachel said. 'The newspaper said so.'

'I know … but the guards will let me in. They all know me. They know I'm the police surgeon. I'm the one who will cut the corpses down tomorrow morning and declare them dead … if I don't save them first.'

Rachel's petticoats and skirt dragged at her legs as she tried to keep up with the rushing Doctor. Now was the dangerous hour when people in Lawnmarket and Castlehill were emptying their chamber pots into the street and covering careless passers-by in human filth.

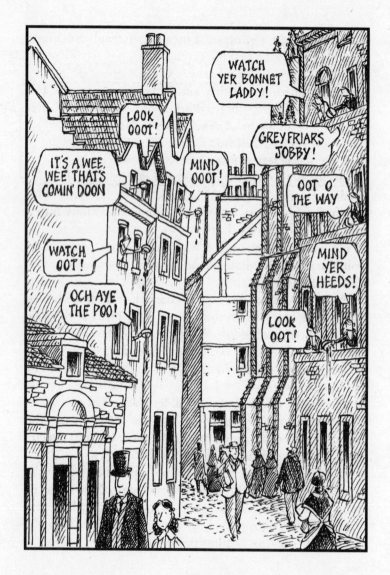

114

Doctor Bell marched through the gates of the Castle like a knight riding to the rescue.

I know knights didn't wear shiny top hats ... at least I don't think they did. And they didn't wear black tailcoats and fine grey trousers. But if they DID they would look like the brave young, clever young, handsome young Doctor.

As he passed the Castle's Great Hall he nodded towards it. 'That's where the Earl of Douglas was executed,' he said.

'Hanged? In the Great Hall?'

'No, he was butchered. King James II was just nine years old and he invited young Earl Douglas and his brother to dinner. The Keeper of the Castle marched in and placed the bloody head of a bull on the table in front of Earl Douglas.'

'To eat?'

'No, it was uncooked – it was an old Scottish sign that the Earl was to die. The young King screamed he wouldn't allow it. But Earl Douglas was dragged out and hacked to death along with his brother. Douglas was only sixteen and his brother was younger. It was known as the 'Black Dinner' and they say the Castle has been cursed ever since for the dreadful deed. They say a minstrel sang that he hoped the Castle would sink into the ground.'

'I've heard the verse.' Rachel nodded. She recited it as they walked past the ghastly site.

'Edinburgh Castle, town and tower,
  God grant that you sink for your sin.'

'A vicious execution,' Doctor Bell sighed.

Then Rachel said something she should not have said. It would come back to haunt her like the ghosts of butchered boys.

'Not an execution … a murder.'

Doctor Bell did one of his sudden stops. He turned and looked down over the town with its beads of gas lights strung along streets like a glittering necklace. Rachel held her breath as Doctor Bell began to speak. 'Not an execution … a murder,' he said. 'There is something there … some clue to this mystery.' He shook his head. 'I wish I weren't so tired. I can't think. I can't think. But the answer is there somewhere.'

He went on to the prison block where Bairn and Kitty Bruce lay without even a candle to keep them warm.

It was as dark as their lives. Doomed to end the next morning.

SPIDER, SECRET AND SEWER-PIPE

Kitty Bruce woke up with an aching head. Her gin bottle was dry and she couldn't find the laudanum she always carried.

'Are you all right, Aunt Kitty?' Bairn asked as they lay in the cell, lit only with a little starlight.

The woman shook her head. 'I've been better. I'll be glad when I get out of here. This cell stinks.'

Bairn nodded. 'It was full of thieves and beggars. They let them go. But we're here because we are supposed to hang in the morning.'

'Hah!' the old woman laughed. 'Kitty Bruce was never born to hang ... and neither were you, Bairn.'

'So you said. But we only have twelve hours to find a way out of this,' the boy said.

'I am a *Bruce*!' Kitty crowed suddenly. 'You know what that means? The Bruce family used to rule Scotland. I have royal blood in my veins. Not only that but the Bruces are fighters. Remember Robert the Bruce?'

'Was that your father? I never met him,' the boy said.

'No! Robert the Bruce was one of the great Kings of Scotland. It's said he was down and defeated six times by his enemies. He hid in a cave. While he was there he saw a spider spinning a web. He watched her as she tried to throw her thread from one edge of the cave wall to another. Six times she fell short. 'Ah, you poor wee thing!' Robert sighed. 'I know what it's like to fall six times in a row.' But the brave spider didn't give up. It tried a seventh time.' Kitty smiled.

'And it failed again?'

'No! It reached the other side and finished its web. Robert took heart when he saw that. He gathered his armies and the seventh time he won back the throne of Scotland. There's a lesson there for you and me, Bairn!'

'What?' the boy puzzled. 'You want us to weave a web and catch flies?'

'No! The lesson is, never give up – even when all is lost. Go into battle crying, "A Bruce! A Bruce!" and anything can happen.'

And it was then that a candle shone in at the steel grille on the door and the cell door opened. 'See?' Kitty cackled. 'Rescue!'

Kitty and Bairn rose to their feet and watched as Rachel entered the cell with Doctor Bell. 'Good evening, Bairn,' the girl said with a warm smile. 'You've met Doctor Bell.'

The Doctor nodded at the criminal couple in front of him and said, 'I've travelled a long way to meet you, Kitty Bruce.'

'I shouldn't be here,' Kitty cried.

'Yes, you should,' Doctor Bell said sternly. 'Children in your care have died – at least four that the Dundee police know of.'

The old woman dropped her gaze to the rushes on the floor. 'Babies die. It's what they do best. Dying. The best-loved, best-cared-for baby can die. I can't be blamed. I never killed them ... never smothered them the way those woman did in England. That Margaret Walters ... and the one that killed fifty in London...'

Tragic but true, especially in the filth of Queen Victoria's slums. For once Kitty Bruce was telling the plain truth – except when she said dying was what they do best. They cry and make nasty smells better than anything on the planet.

'Baby farming is illegal,' Doctor Bell said firmly. 'You will be transported to Australia for it, that's for sure.'

'I'd rather hang,' the woman spat.

'And blackmail,' Rachel reminded the Doctor. 'You thought Miss Bruce had a secret she was using to get money from someone, didn't you, Doctor Bell? She could hang for that?'

'Perhaps,' he said. 'So, Kitty Bruce, are you going to tell me about the blackmail? The secret?'

Kitty gave a choking laugh. 'What? After that lassie just said I'd hang for it? I don't know any secrets ... and I'm not a murderer. I should be free. And so should the boy, you know. Whoever sent him to hang was a cruel, cruel woman.'

'I don't know which magistrate it was,' Doctor Bell admitted. 'You're right – it's too harsh. But I can't argue with a magistrate – not unless I have proof. And Bairn can't tell me anything that will help – he can't even tell me that Bill Twist *forced* him to go down the chimney. You don't remember, do you. Bairn?'

'I remember the back lane … I had an odd feeling there was someone in the shadows…'

'The youth,' Doctor Bell nodded. 'I guessed he'd be involved.'

'And I remember waking up in the cell with you looking at my head wound. But I just don't remember the bit in between,' Bairn groaned.

'So, you'll come and watch us hang, will you, Doctor Bell?' Kitty asked. 'Then you'll carry us to the surgeons in Edinburgh and watch them cut us up?'

The medical school in Edinburgh was famous for teaching doctors how the human body works. And they did it by cutting up corpses. Corpses of the hanged were always cut up. Fifty years before Bairn was born, poor Edinburgh people of West Port and Grassmarket were murdered by William Burke and William Hare to sell fresh bodies to the surgeons. But that's another story …

In the faint light of the candle Doctor Bell looked pained. He held the keys to the cell in his hand. The guard had given them to the Doctor and left him to enter then lock up afterwards.

'Tell me your secret and I can help you,' he urged.

'A Bruce!' Kitty cried suddenly. 'I'm a Bruce and we don't give in.'

Doctor Bell shook his head and turned suddenly. 'Let's

leave them, Rachel,' he said.

'Goodbye,' the girl said softly to Bairn. 'I'll be in the Lawnmarket tomorrow when they hang you.'

The boy grinned. 'I wasn't born to hang,' he told her. 'I wasn't.'

Poor boy. Rachel took out a handkerchief and seemed to be crying into it as she left the cell. That's why she didn't see quite what happened next. Doctor Bell placed the key in the cell door and rattled it. Of course Rachel thought he'd locked Bairn and Kitty in. In fact he just rattled the key ... but didn't turn it.

Rachel didn't know the cell door was unlocked and the two prisoners inside were free to slip out. She left the Doctor and went home to sleep. She needed to be awake early if she was going to catch the hanging. She'd wear her best black dress and carry her fine black, silk parasol. She'd even have a black lace handkerchief to dab away the tears ... if she could force her eyes to squeeze out some tears that is.

But as she slipped into her warm bed that night she didn't know that the cell door in the Castle was about to open. Bairn and Kitty had seen exactly what the Doctor had done – even if they didn't understand why.

***

Kitty clutched the bars and tugged. The heavy door swung open easily. The passage was lit by a single gas lamp. All the other cell doors were open and empty.

A clock struck midnight and the sounds of the distant town were more snores than drunken roars now.

The two prisoners crept to the end of the corridor and an archway led on to the battlements. Below them guards wandered around lazily, some smoked pipes and some drank ale. Even the laziest guard would stop them if they walked down the steps into the courtyard or tried to leave by the main gate on to Castlehill.

'We're out of the cell but we can't get out of the Castle,' Bairn murmured.

'A Bruce never gives up!' Kitty said in a creaking voice. 'We can't go out of the gate ... but we can go over the wall,' she said.

Bairn frowned. He looked over the battlements. Kings Stables Road was a long way below. A line of gas lamps on the road gave a faint light up there. It showed gaps in the wall stones where he could grip with his toes. Then a toilet pipe ran down over the cliffs to the sewer-pipes on the ground. It was easier than climbing a chimney, Bairn knew.

'I could get down ... Izzie told me how ... but I'm not leaving you,' he said.

'Leaving me!' Kitty almost screamed and pushed her knuckles into her mouth as guards below turned to look up. She sank back into the shadows. 'Leaving me?' she said more softly. 'I should think you're *not* leaving me! I'm coming with you.'

'You might fall ... and if you did you'd be killed,' Bairn told her.

Kitty threw back her head in a silent laugh. 'And I could stay here nice and safe ... and be hanged in front of twenty thousand jeering jackasses. No, my boy, I'm light as Robert the Bruce's spider and I'm sure I can do it. But a Bruce would rather die trying than give up. You go first ... guide my feet into the cracks, if you want to help me.'

'I will,' Bairn said and pulled himself up on to the top of the wall. He reached out a hand and lifted Kitty Bruce alongside him.

He was about to lower himself over the wall when Kitty stopped him. 'Bairn ... if I fall and hurt myself don't worry. Save yourself. Run as fast and as far as you can. You have a vicious enemy in Edinburgh. You have to escape her clutches.'

'Who?' he asked. 'I haven't any enemies. Who, Kitty?'
'Your mother,' she said. 'Now go.'

***

The cool April air made the climb a joy for the boy. It was like no chimney he'd ever been in … it was more like the trees he'd climbed in Dundee with the other children. Behind him Kitty's feet were strong and the air made her feel younger than her ragged grey hair made her look. 'If I live through this I'll give up the gin,' she swore.

They reached the bottom of the Castle wall and Bairn began to look for a way down the cliff. The toilet pipe gave a fine hold for their hands and the cliff face was full of shelves for their feet that let them climb down easily.

They were the height of two men from the bottom when the cliff became smooth as glass and there were no footholds. 'We'll have to just slide down the pipe,' Bairn called up.

'Do it then, boy,' the woman said.

Bairn held on to the pipe and gracefully slid to the grass at the bottom of the cliff and looked up. Kitty gripped the pipe with one hand and then the other. She tried to wrap a foot around the pipe but there was nothing to grip on to. All her weight was held by her arms … and the arms were weary from the climb.

She felt the ache in her shoulders and wrists turn to pain and her fingers opened.

Kitty Bruce fell.

BOMB, BRIDGE AND BOWL

In the light of a distant gas lamp Bairn saw Kitty fall. He stretched out his thin but strong arms to catch her, or at least break her fall. But the woman twisted in the air and she landed on the boy's head before tumbling to the grass. The pain in his head made him dizzy for a while.

They lay side by side for a while, moaning. 'Anything broken?' Bairn asked once he'd stopped feeling dizzy from the blow to his head.

'Yes,' Kitty whined. 'Me gin bottle!'

'I mean any bones? Can you walk?'

'Walk? Where to?'

'The only people I know in Edinburgh who might help us are Bill Twist and Miss Rachel!'

'Not young Rachel!' Kitty said sharply. 'I'd rather trust a cheat, a liar and a villain any day. Besides, Bill Twist owes you a favour for keeping him off the gallows. You didn't betray him as your master.'

A dreadful thing to say. YOU would trust young Rachel, wouldn't you?

'And I didn't betray the Fenians,' Bairn said as he rose

126

to his feet and helped Kitty up.

'Fenians? The men who're plotting to kill the Queen?' Kitty asked. 'What do you know about them?'

'Everything,' Bairn said softly. 'I was in the room while they made their plans … then one of them smacked me over the head with a club and I forgot everything I'd heard.'

'Then I just smacked you over the head when I fell,' Kitty cackled, 'and you got your memory back!'

Bairn sighed. 'But we can't do anything about it. If we go to the police to report the Fenians, they'll take us straight to the gallows.'

Kitty stood as tall as she could and the night breeze blew her hair back from her face. She looked like an avenging eagle. 'I am a Bruce … I could be Queen of Scotland, you know! I will not let the Queen of England be killed in my land!'

'We can't go to the police,' Bairn repeated.

'No. But we don't need the police … we stop the plot ourselves. Now, where does this Bill Twist live?'

'Over his shop in the High Street.'

'Then we'll go there and make our plans,' the woman said and trotted ahead of Bairn towards the Lawnmarket.

They walked under the shadow of the gallows at St Giles and into the High Street. The sky was turning a pale shade of pearl grey ahead of them as the day began to break. There were just two hours to go before they were due to hang. Four hours before Victoria was due to be blown into mincemeat.

Victoria was a fat lady. Sorry, it has to be said. The mincemeat would be very fatty mincemeat. Not the sort you'd enjoy in a Vic-burger – even with grilled cheese on top.

Men, women and children were strolling up the hill with stools. 'I'm tired, Ma!' a little girl of about five whinged.

'Quiet, Bessie. If we're nice and early we'll get our seats right in the front row. That'll be nice, won't it?'

'I suppose so, Ma,' the girl muttered and walked on.

Kitty snorted. 'Sorry to disappoint you!' she muttered.

***

The people of Edinburgh were stirring. But they weren't out as early as Rachel was.

She couldn't sleep for the thought of Bairn sitting in the Castle, waiting to die. She wanted it all over with.

Doctor Bell had left her at her house but she didn't even go to bed. She went down to the kitchen and took a large pie from the pantry. They say the person who is about to hang should have a good breakfast.

Rachel told her coachman to get the horses ready and drive her up to the Castle again. 'I've come to see the prisoners,' she told the guard.

He shrugged and led the way down the dank passage to the cell. He thrust the key into the lock and tried to turn it. 'Funny,' he said, 'It won't turn.' He twisted it the other way and the lock clicked. 'Ohhhh!' he breathed. 'It's already open.'

'If your prisoners have escaped then you will be shot, I expect,' Rachel sneered, her eyes glinting. 'Or even better – you will take their place on the gallows in a few hours' time.'

He scowled at the girl. 'It wasn't my fault. I left the keys with Doctor Bell ... he must have forgotten to lock the door.'

'No use blaming someone else,' she said and made the sign of a noose being tight round his neck. 'Cccct!'

He pulled open the door and looked inside. The cell was empty. 'They didn't walk past me at the gatehouse,' he said angrily. 'And no one ever escapes from Edinburgh Castle.'

'That's not true,' the girl said. 'Everyone's heard the story that raiders once climbed in and cut the throats of idle guards like you. And one guard used to climb down to see his girlfriend,' she told him.

'Impossible,' the soldier said.

'They used the toilet pipe.'

Rachel ran to the wall and looked over. On the grass, far below she saw two figures sitting. She watched as they began walking towards the Lawnmarket. They would need to hide, she knew. Bairn had just two friends in Edinburgh he could turn to for help – Bill Twist and herself. If he had walked North up King's Stables Road he'd have been going to her house.

He wasn't. So he must be heading for Twist's home. Rachel turned and ran past the guard and out of the gate. She ordered the coach to take her down Castlehill. They passed the gallows where people were already gathering.

Rachel stepped down at the corner of World's End and sent the coachman home. She rattled on the door of Bill Twist's shop.

The little man with the bald head and pixie ears was already awake and looking ill. 'Miss Rachel … oh, what have I done?' he groaned. 'I've let young Bairn go to the gallows in my place! Look, the crowds are gathering already.'

'Don't worry, Mr Twist … you may be in for a surprise before the sun comes up!'

***

Bairn tapped on the door of Bill Twist's shop and stepped back in surprise when Rachel opened it. Her smile was warm but her gaze was steely. 'Come in, Bairn. I've been expecting you.'

He hurried into the safety of the shadows of the shop and pulled Kitty Bruce after him. 'Expecting me?'

'Ever since I persuaded Doctor Bell to leave your cell door open. I knew a clever climber like you would get free.'

A lie? Are you calling Rachel a liar? Oh, I suppose you NEVER tell lies? Of course you do. So a little fib like that does no one any harm.

'Thank you, Miss Rachel,' he said.

The girl led the way up the stairs to Bill's kitchen where he was boiling water on his gas stove to make tea for them.

'Now I suppose you want help to escape from Edinburgh, do you?' Bill put in.

'No,' Kitty Bruce said, 'first we have to save the Queen!'

Rachel cut the pie and shared it around while Bill Twist poured tea and Bairn told his amazing story. The story of the Fenians, Sunday, Tuesday and Thursday, and the North Bridge bomb plot.

'So we tell Detective Chief Inspector Gott,' Rachel said.

'No police,' Kitty Bruce spat. 'We'll do this ourselves.'

'You can't just walk on to North Bridge and snatch the bomb away from these desperate men,' the girl argued. 'Bairn's just told us that the American has a revolver. He'll shoot you before you get within ten paces!'

'No,' the cunning old woman grinned. 'He would shoot a policeman ... or he may even shoot a rich young lady like *you*. But he won't shoot a poor woman like me and a ragged boy like Bairn. We can get close.'

Rachel shook her head. 'As soon as you try to snatch the bomb they'll see you are out to spoil their plan – poor or not, they would shoot you,' she argued.

Bairn wiped pie crumbs from his chin and grinned. 'I have an idea,' he said. 'As soon as they drop the bomb they will have to duck out of the way of the blast. That's the moment we can make a run for it.'

'You *can't* let them drop the bomb!' Rachel cried.

Bairn laughed. 'It won't be a bomb they are dropping. That's the clever part of my plan...'

***

Daylight came and the fearless four were ready with Bairn's plan. Still there were two hours to wait before the train arrived. They looked out of the window into High Street where crowds of angry people were heading down the hill. Angry because they had been cheated of their hanging.

An officer from the Castle stood on the scaffold and told them there would be no execution that day. He tried to tell them there was a reward of a hundred pounds if anyone could capture the escaped prisoners. The mob howled in fury and someone cried out they should hang the officer instead. It took a troop of Castle guards with rifles to rescue him.

One of Bill Twist's many clocks chimed quarter to ten and they got ready to go and save the Queen of Britain and the British Empire.

Of course Vic wasn't happy with being a queen when her own daughter in Germany was about to become empress ... and being empress is posher than being queen so that would never do. So in 1877 Victoria made herself Empress of India AS WELL as Queen of Britain! She'll go on to be the poshest lady in the world ... if Bairn can save her.

Bairn picked up a goldfish bowl that had been for sale in Bill Twist's shop. Now it was filled with soot. It looked like a shiny black globe – the same size as the iron bomb Bairn had seen in the dining room at 23 George Street.

He dressed in some of Bill Twist's clothes and used more soot to blacken his face – he did not want anyone to see him and claim the hundred pounds reward. Kitty Bruce placed a shawl over her head and wrapped it over her mouth so her face was hidden too.

They placed their bomb in a gift box and stepped out into the empty street. All of Edinburgh was at the station hoping to catch a glimpse of the Queen. A policemen stood, bored, on the end of North Bridge. Kitty Bruce, Queen of Scotland, gave a sign for Rachel to stay there with Bill Twist.

Three men were already on the bridge, looking towards the morning sun in the east and waiting for the train.

There was a tall giant of a man with a fine suit – Sunday, Kitty guessed from what Bairn had told them. A weedy man in a black suit – Tuesday - and an old man with a tragic face and ragged clothes … Thursday

Bairn and Kitty Bruce hurried over to them.

***

Sunday saw the boy and the woman walking quickly towards them and reached inside his coat to rest a hand on his revolver. 'Good day,' he drawled in his rich, American voice.

'Sunday?' Kitty said.

The three men looked confused. 'Who are you?' Thursday asked.

'I am Wednesday and the boy is Friday,' Kitty said. 'There has been a small change of plan.'

'But … but … where are you from?'

Bairn chirped, 'Your brothers in Manchester sent us to help. We have a newer, better bomb for you.'

Sunday opened his mouth to argue but suddenly heard the shriek of a train whistle. They could see the plume of white smoke from the engine.

'Why did no one tell me?' Sunday roared.

'There are traitors about. Messages get into the wrong hands,' Kitty said.

'I suppose so,' the American nodded. 'Is your bomb ready to light?'

'All we need is a fuse,' Bairn said. 'We were told to use yours.'

The boy opened the box and pulled out the goldfish

bowl bomb. The train was closer now and time was running out. Thursday opened his coat and they could see the iron bomb. He tugged the fuse out and handed it to Bairn. The boy quickly pushed it in to the soot and turned to hold the bowl over the side of the bridge. Tuesday held the matches ready. Sunday began to count as the train came nearer, slowing down all the time. When the engine reached the bridge the smoke hid them. 'Light it!' Sunday cried.

The engine passed beneath them. Tuesday struck a match and lit the fuse. The first coach passed under the bridge. 'Three…' Sunday barked. Then the second coach. 'Two …' Then the Queen's coach. 'One … and drop it!'

Bairn released the soot bomb. The three Fenians dived for shelter under the bridge.

There was a faint tinkle of glass.

Bairn and Kitty were already racing towards the policeman standing at the end of the bridge.

'Arrest those men!' Kitty cried. The Fenians scrambled to their feet and ran off the other way. 'Go on, officer, catch them!' she cried.

The officer ignored her pleas as he took a pair of handcuffs from his belt and snapped one link on Kitty's wrist and the other on Bairn. 'Kitty Bruce and Bairn Bruce – I arrest you in the name of the law … and Edinburgh will have its hanging today after all!'

MURDER, MYSTERY AND MACKAYS

'**D**octor Bell,' said Queen Victoria as she looked through the carriage window. 'We are pleased to see you again. It will be good to have you at Balmoral with us. One has a small twinge of pain in one's knee we wish you to look at.'

Doctor Bell bowed and was about to step into the carriage when Chief Inspector Gott waddled along the platform, red-faced and panting. 'Ah, Bell! Just caught you in time ... the Fenians ... the Fenians tried to strike from North Bridge. We have the villains on their way to the court now. It was that couple that escaped the hanging!'

The Doctor quickly explained what had happened to the shocked Queen and she nodded. 'Ah, then you must indeed go to court and see justice done. You may follow us to Balmoral tomorrow.'

The Doctor bowed again and hurried to the cab that Gott had waiting. Rachel had hurried home straight after the fake bomb had been thrown because she had an urgent message for her mother. Doctor Bell went to the cell at the police station. He was there a long while.

The Doctor heard the full story from Kitty and Bairn – pretty much the story you have just read. He closed his eyes and blew out a long breath. 'I am the biggest fool in Edinburgh,' he said. 'Now I see what has happened. Now I know who has been pulling the strings behind this puppet show – the strings that almost led you to dance on Mr Calcraft's gallows. Now I see who the shadow youth is – the one who made the wicked plot work.'

'Can you save us?' Kitty Bruce asked.

Doctor Bell walked to the cell door and looked through the iron bars. Constable Donald stood there with the keys. 'Is the magistrate ready to hear the case?' the Doctor asked.

'Yes, sir.'

'And who is the magistrate this morning?'

'Lady Mackay, sir.'

Doctor Bell gave a wide grin and turned back to the baby farmer. 'In that case, I *can* save you!'

Bairn nodded with relief. 'You were right, Aunt Kitty … I wasn't born to hang!'

***

'This court will rise,' Mr Pickles said and everyone stood up as Lady Ethel Mackay entered and took her seat. Doctor Bell sat beside Chief Inspector Gott and Constable

Donald. From time to time the Constable rattled his handcuffs as if he were waiting to use them. Rachel sat in her usual seat at the back of the court and watched to see poor Bairn's last hour of life before he was led to the scaffold.

Lady Mackay was wearing the hat with the heavy veil again. She waved a hand towards Kitty Bruce and Bairn and spoke quickly. 'These two villains have tried to assassinate the Queen. For that they should hang ... but it hardly matters. I will not hold a trial on the charge of throwing a bomb at the Queen's train. They are due to hang anyway. The scaffold is already built. No need to wait till dawn tomorrow to execute them. Have it done now, Mr Gott,' she said and rose to her feet.

Doctor Bell jumped from his seat. 'Excuse me, Lady Mackay, but I wish to speak on behalf of the accused.'

The magistrate gave a hoarse laugh and said, 'NOT the accused – the condemned.'

The Doctor leaned forward on the table in front of him. 'I will speak anyway,' he said.

'How *dare* you ...' Lady Mackay began to roar but the Doctor cut her off with soft words.

'My Lady, Kitty Bruce is accused of child cruelty and the boy is accused of burglary ... and they are both accused of dropping a bowl of soot on the royal train. But there is a far more serious charge to bring before this court. The charge of attempted murder, My Lady.'

Lady Mackay spread her hands, 'Then let us hear it, Doctor Bell. It will pass the time till lunch – I always like to watch a hanging after a good meal. Which miserable wretch is accused of attempted murder.'

The Doctor stood up straight and raised his right arm. He pointed a fine finger. 'You are, Lady Mackay. I accuse you.'

The magistrate raised her veil and her eyes were the hot burning red that flashed when she was angry. 'I will have you locked away for so long you will forget what freedom is, Doctor Bell ...' she began to growl. Again he cut her off.

'I will tell the true story about your evil plan, Lady Mackay. You and your cunning partner in crime. You will sit there and listen while Constable Donald makes notes. You will have a fair and proper trial at a later date ... unlike the one you gave Bairn and his Aunt Kitty. Now sit down and listen, Lady Mackay, or I will have Constable Donald handcuff you to the rails of the dock.'

The magistrate sank into her chair and refused to look at the Doctor. She stared straight ahead towards the back of the court where Rachel sat.

Doctor Bell took a deep breath and began. 'Our story starts in 1855. Miss Ethel Scrogg fell in love with a shopkeeper who sold antiques. Then she discovered he was in fact a thief who sold stolen goods. She left him and met a Colonel Mackay. Then she discovered she was having the shopkeeper's baby. She went to Dundee and, in 1856, gave birth to the baby. She handed it over to Kitty Bruce, the baby farmer. She returned to Edinburgh and married Colonel Mackay. They went off to India with the Army and had a daughter two years later.'

Bairn gasped, 'So Lady Mackay is my mother?' and he looked with horror at the horse-faced magistrate. Lady

Mackay did not seem to hear him.

Doctor Bell went on. 'Kitty Bruce raised the child, Bairn, to be a sweep's boy and brought him to Edinburgh to sell him in 1862 when he was six. She also decided to call on Lady Mackay and ask for money. If Her Ladyship wanted to keep quiet about the boy then she would have to pay Kitty. But Lady Mackay was still in India. So Miss Bruce waited till this year to visit Edinburgh again. She visited Lady Mackay and demanded money. Isn't that right?'

'A thousand pounds,' the magistrate whispered.

'She sent the baby farmer away with twenty pounds in gold and the promise of more. That was when you, Lady Ethel Mackay, came up with a plan. A plan to kill your son, Bairn. If the boy was dead Kitty Bruce would have no hold over her. So Lady Mackay sent a youth with a message to the sweep. She wanted Bairn to clean a chimney in a house in the New Town. When Bairn appeared the young lady of the house would, of course, take Bairn away from the sweep. He was offered to Mr Bill Twist – a burglar. Then all Lady Mackay had to do was make sure Bairn was caught doing a burglary. She sent her young messenger to Mr Twist with a message – 'Rob number 23 George Street this evening and you will find silver there'. The youth then followed Twist and Bairn to make sure they did the robbery. As soon as Bairn went down the chimney the youth ran to the police and told them where they could catch him.'

'And we did,' Chief Inspector Gott muttered.

'Lady Mackay made sure that she was the magistrate on the case the next morning. She couldn't believe her luck when she found Kitty Bruce had been arrested too. She sentenced them *both* to death! Like the Black Dinner!'

Rachel stirred at mention of the Black Dinner. That was the clue she had given to Doctor Bell by mistake – she said the killing in the Castle wasn't an execution – it was a murder.

And that was what Lady Mackay had tried. She had tried to use the gallows to kill her enemy. It wasn't an execution it was a murder. The hangman would do the killing for her – she would use the law for murder.

Doctor Bell continued. 'As soon as Bairn and Kitty Bruce were hanged, Lady Mackay's secret would be safe. Of course she didn't want Bill Twist to be hanged for being Bairn's boss – you see, Bill Twist was the lawless shop-keeper she had loved all those years ago – Bill Twist is the father of Bairn. Lady Mackay's messenger made sure Bairn stayed quiet about Bill.'

Lady Mackay moved suddenly. Her eyes burned and her hand slammed down on the bench she sat at. 'Nonsense, Doctor Bell. You cannot prove one word of this. This … this *youth* you talk about. You have not caught him. You have no idea what he looks like. He doesn't exist. He is just a shadow. Nothing more!'

'A girl has been with me while I followed clues around Edinburgh. She saw the youth clearly – she described his twisted smile and his clothes. For twelve precious hours that put me off the scent – twelve hours in which Bairn and Kitty could have hanged. Luckily they escaped and saved their own lives … they also saved the life of Queen Victoria. I think you'll find that the Queen will pardon

Bairn's little burglaries. And Kitty too – no one can be sure the babies died from cruelty.'

'They didn't,' the woman said. 'Babies die. It's what they do best.'

'Doctor Bell,' Lady Mackay said fiercely. 'I have listened to enough of your nonsense. You are clever. You should be a detective. But you have not one piece of *proof* of this fantastic story.'

The police officers, Bairn and Kitty turned towards him in wonder.

'Where?' Constable Donald asked and rattled his handcuffs again.

Doctor Bell said, 'It is your daughter, Lady Mackay. The daughter born in India. The daughter who had so much to lose if Kitty Bruce told the world you had another child – a son. Your daughter helped drag this poor couple into the very shadow of the gallows.'

'Pah!' the magistrate snorted like a horse. 'The youth is a boy – you said so yourself … the girl that was with you saw him.'

'No, she *said* she saw him. She wanted to fool me and she did. Because the girl *is* the youth, isn't she, Lady Mackay?' He turned round slowly to gaze at the back row of the seats in court. 'Your daughter helped you in your murder plot.' He was looking at Rachel and smiling sadly. 'Isn't that right, Rachel Mackay?' he asked her.

Of course you'd worked that out ... hadn't you? There were enough clues in the story. In fact you probably worked it out before Doctor Bell which means you are a proper little Sherlock Holmes. That's odd. If you don't mind my saying, you don't look that clever.

ENDINGS

1875

Rachel was sentenced to seven years' transportation to Australia for her part in Lady Mackay's wicked plot. Now seven years had passed and she was on the ship heading back to Leith port.

Rachel's mother was sentenced to fourteen years transportation. Her father was so ashamed he divorced Lady Mackay and would not agree to see Rachel again.

Never mind, Rachel had a trusty half-brother called Bairn. He had become quite a hero in Edinburgh since his soot-bowl plot saved the Queen. He ran a very honest trinket shop in the High Street with his father, Mr William Twist. The shadow of the gallows had been hanging over Twist and it had frightened him badly. With his son's help he changed his twisted ways ...mostly.

Rachel was sure Bairn and Bill would look after her till she was ready to find a rich fool to marry her. Why shouldn't she? Her mother had! And Rachel *was* the girl who helped save the Queen, wasn't she?

She looked over the side of the ship as it drifted home and dreamed. She would have a fine house in the New Town.

The ship headed up the Firth of Forth now and she could see the grey haze that always hung over Old Reekie. She was sure there'd be many things that had changed.

That year *another* law had been passed to stop boys being sent up chimneys. They believed this law would really work … but they said that last time!

And they had stopped hanging people in public – the Fenian, Michael Barrett was the last. He died in 1868. He became a martyr, of course, and the Fenians were stronger than ever.

The Mackays were among the last ever convicts to be sent to Australia, the other side of the world.

Rachel's ship bumped into the quay at Leith docks. Criminals coming home didn't have friends to welcome them back. The quayside was empty.

Except for one young man. He looked about twenty years old. He had a fine suit and was handsome. He wasn't very tall for his age and he'd never grow much more.

He was looking up towards Rachel as the sailors threw the ropes to the dock workers and hauled them gently towards the quay.

Criminals didn't have friends to welcome them back home. But Rachel did.

The young man was smiling and waving.

She waved back screaming, 'Bairn! Oh, Bairn you've forgiven me!'

He nodded.

'I am Rachel Mackay,' she said fiercely, 'and I am home.'

Edinburgh ... beware.

EPILOGUE

The story is a mixture of real people and imagined –
real crimes and imagined.

Of course Queen Victoria really lived in those
days and enjoyed her summer holiday at Balmoral Castle
in the north of Scotland. There were eight attempts to
assassinate her ... but NOT the Fenian plot in this story.
In 1901 Victoria ... by the Grace of God, of the United
Kingdom of Great Britain and Ireland Queen, Defender
of the Faith, Empress of India ... died. She was assassinated
by that deadly killer, old age.

And her Scottish doctor *was* Doctor Joseph Bell.

What you might NOT know is Doctor Bell is
remembered for another reason. In 1877 a student doctor
went to classes run by Doctor Bell and was amazed at
what a detective brain Joseph Bell had. The student was
called Arthur Conan Doyle. Young Arthur did not go on
to be a doctor. He took up writing. He created the most
famous detective ever, Sherlock Holmes. Arthur said
Sherlock is based on Joseph Brainy Bell!

Baby farmers did take unwanted children for money.
Good baby farmers found homes for the children. Evil
baby farmers simply let the babies die or 'helped' them to
die.

The Fenians carried on with their violence, killing and
dying for a free Ireland. Michael Barrett was the last man
hanged in public for his part in the Clerkenwell Jail

bombing ... even though he may have been in Glasgow at the time. The Fenians were a strong force in the USA but the three men described in this story were invented.

Edinburgh Castle exists, of course – and the horrors of the Black Dinner and the Thomas Randolf raid are true. It looks impossible to climb those cliffs but it can be done ... and William Frank really did climb OUT of the Castle to visit his girlfriend, so the escape in this story is possible.

You can visit Edinburgh and the streets named in the story. There are so many more true and terrible tales Old Reekie can tell. Visit St Giles where so many criminals met a horrible end.

Stand in the shadow of the church and you are standing in the shadow of the gallows...

If you enjoyed Shadow of
the Gallows, then you'll love
three more Gory Stories,
written by Terry Deary.
Why not read the
whole horrible lot?

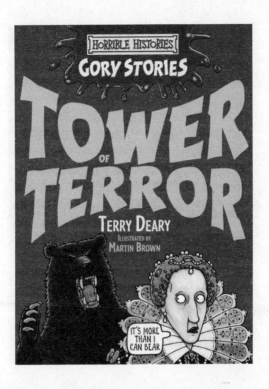

Simon Tuttle and his Pa are tricksters struggling to make a living on the Tudor streets. When disaster strikes Simon must fend for himself, even if it means committing treason. But can he pull off his Pa's carefully concocted plan and should he trust his mysterious new accomplice?

Find out in this Terrible Tudor adventure, it's got all the gore and so much more!

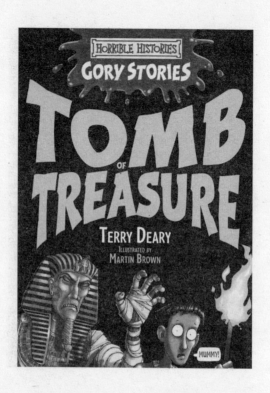

Phoul Pharaoh Tutankhamun has died and is about to be buried. It's master-thief Antef's big moment – can he and his crew of criminals pull off the biggest grave-robbery of all time and empty Tut's tomb of its richest treasures?

Find out in this Awful Egyptian adventure, it's got all the gore and so much more!

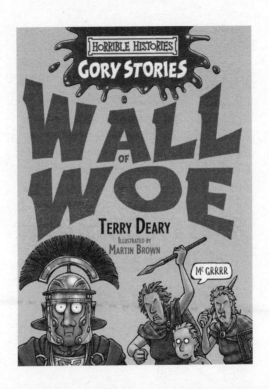

A wild and wind-lashed wall separates two terrifying tribes: the Picts and the Britons. Two Gaul soldiers are given the task of guarding the wall – on pain of death. But with catapults, feasts and football to distract them, will they be able to keep the peace and solve the mystery of the lost legion?

Find out in this Rotten Roman adventure, it's got all the gore and so much more!

**Here's a terrifying taster
of Tower of Terror, a
Tudor gory story...**

BLOOD, BUCKETS AND BOARDS

Simon!' Master Thomas Tuttle shouted. 'Go and get me a bucket of blood.'

'Yes, Pa,' the scawny boy said wearily. They were staying at the Lewes Inn in Southwark. It was a rat-infested, damp and stinking hole. The landlord put bowls of goat's blood on the bedroom floor to attract the fleas and keep them off the sleeping guests. Every morning he drowned a hundred fleas but every night their friends came back to bite his guests.

Still, the inn was cheap and close to the south end of London Bridge and the Bear Gardens where the Tuttles had just done their show.

Simon rose from the straw, brushed the fleas off his tunic and stepped over the snoring drunks he and his Pa shared the room with. He took the bearskin cloak that he used for a blanket and threw it over his shoulders. It was cold in the tavern – it would be colder outside.

The boy tumbled down the dark stairway and into Tooley Street. He collected a slops bucket from behind the door and turned east towards Gully Hole and the butcher shop. He pushed through a flock of bleating sheep that were on their way to the butcher and licked his lips. 'I'll be having a bit of you for my supper tonight!' he jeered at a black-faced lamb, but the lamb didn't believe him. All he replied was, 'Bah!'

An icy wind stung his face but at least the cold would kill the plague. Well, that's what Pa used to say. In the summer, when the stink was higher than the Tower of London, the bad air could kill you inside a day.

'First you feel dizzy and your head aches,' Doctor Lamp used to tell them in the tavern. 'Then you get a cough. And when you start coughing blood there's no hope for you. You'll be feeding the worms in the churchyard before the day is out!' He would wave a warning finger under their noses. 'And if you see anyone coughing blood just take to your heels and run.'

'Can you really catch the plague from blood?' Simon asked him.

The Doctor fixed the boy with his watery eyes. 'I've seen it many a time. When I was your age, young Simon, I caught the plague and I got over it. I was one of the lucky ones. Once you get over it you never catch it again. That's how I came to be a doctor and brought comfort to the plague victims. That's why there's no one better!' he boasted.

Why did Simon believe him? If Doctor Lamp was that good he should have been the richest man in London. But he was as ragged and skinny as a parson's cat and smelled even worse. His white beard was thinner than the east wind and his bones poked through his clothes. Simon believed Doctor Lamp when he said blood spread the plague. He believed his Pa when he said rotten summer air spread the plague. He believed everyone … and woke each morning thinking it would be his last.

Every time Simon coughed he coughed into his hand ... and looked for spots of blood. He didn't expect to reach the age of 20. His Ma hadn't.

Anyway, I was telling you that Simon set off for the butcher's shop in the freezing morning air. The cobbles were slippery with ice and frozen sheep droppings and he slithered along to Master Ketch the butcher.

Simon was more scared of Master Ketch than he was of the plague. The butcher's forehead was so low his eyebrows disappeared into his black hair. His skin was as yellow as ox fat and his hands as big as legs of pork. He spoke in a sort of growl and spat through the gaps in his teeth on to the bloody sheep fleece on his floor.

He'd just killed a bullock and had spilled the steaming guts on to the floor. Simon decided he'd never eat beef again. (It puts you off, seeing that sort of thing.)

'Can I have a bucket of blood, please, Master Ketch?' the boy asked.

'Help yourself. Barrel in the corner,' the man grunted. 'Two pence.'

'Two pence!' Simon squeaked. Master Ketch always made the boy's voice rise in fear. 'It was only a penny yesterday.'

The man waved the vicious butcher knife under the scrawny boy's thin and pointed nose. 'Ah, but now I know what it's for! And it's not for catching fleas! Now I know how your father uses it to trick money out of people. It's my blood – I deserve a share.'

Get your copy of Tower of Terror NOW!

Don't miss these horribly handy Handbooks for all the gore and more!

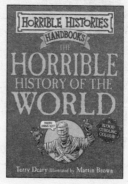

Terry Deary was born at a very early age, so long ago he can't remember. But his mother, who was there at the time, says he was born in Sunderland, north-east England, in 1946 – so it's not true that he writes all *Horrible Histories* from memory. At school he was a horrible child only interested in playing football and giving teachers a hard time. His history lessons were so boring and so badly taught, that he learned to loathe the subject. *Horrible Histories* is his revenge.

Martin Brown was born in Melbourne, on the proper side of the world. Ever since he can remember he's been drawing. His dad used to bring back huge sheets of paper from work and Martin would fill them with doodles and little figures. Then, quite suddenly, with food and water, he grew up, moved to the UK and found work doing what he's always wanted to do: drawing doodles and little figures.